The coachman headed for Hyde Park

Suddenly nervous, Jamaica turned to her companion and said, "Andrew, I must return to Greville House now!"

"You shall, my dear," he replied, "by way of just a short turn in the park. Surely you'll grant me that?" Andrew touched his fingers to her chin, then laid his hand on her cheek. "How cold you are!" he whispered.

Suddenly his mouth was pressed to hers, and Jamaica was lost in an abandoned embrace.

And then, before she had time to struggle or protest, Andrew released his hold and did an astonishing thing.

He buried his handsome head in her lap and broke into loud shuddering sobs!

D1600449

A DEBT OF HONOR
MOLLIE ASHTON

Harlequin Books

TORONTO • NEW YORK • LONDON
AMSTERDAM • PARIS • SYDNEY • HAMBURG
STOCKHOLM • ATHENS • TOKYO • MILAN

Published July 1983
ISBN 0-373-31001-3

Printed in Canada

CHAPTER ONE

THE DUCHESS DROPPED HER LORGNETTE theatrically to emphasize the outrageousness of it all.

"Jamaica! It is unheard of. Quite beyond the pale for a gel of your birth to be gainfully employed."

"Quite, aunt," Jamaica replied, unusually meek. "But I beg you to appreciate my feelings on the subject. I simply cannot expect you to bear the cost of another season for me. I find I am temperamentally unfitted for that—" she faltered only for a moment, then ended boldly "—that mating dance!"

Encouraged by the half-hidden smile that betrayed the duchess's amusement, she continued, "Oh, Aunt Kate, it's so humiliating. Like a horse fair!"

The duchess stroked the black silk cord of the lorgnette studiously. "We try to make it as painless as possible, but pain or pleasure, we must all go through it if we are to make a suitable match." She paused for the statement to take hold. "I don't believe you have given that truth the full consideration it deserves, Jamaica."

"But I have, aunt; truly I have."

"Then I suggest you do so once more." The duchess replaced the lorgnette with slow deliberation and quizzed her niece with a baleful eye.

"Here and now!"

Obediently, Jamaica folded her hands in her lap and

adopted a reflective attitude, as if she were seriously reconsidering her position in life.

There was nothing to reconsider.

Last spring she had had her first taste of the London ton. She recalled the experience with little pleasure. How insufferable those so-called eligible men had been! With forty thousand soldiers lately home from the wars, unemployed and close to starving, all those dandified bucks could think about was the newest cut of their coattails and their interminable gossip of the Prince Regent and his latest amour, one unending discourse after another on Prinny this and Prinny that. And oh, she grimaced at the recollection, their minute, excruciating preoccupation with the knots in their silly cravats!

At the very onset of the season, when she was newly arrived in London, she had to confess it was exciting, even flattering, to be surrounded by elegant gallants at the assemblies and entertainments, all vying to amuse and charm her. It was a far cry from the simple diversions of the West Country. But after a week at Aunt Kate's London house and an unremitting round of social events, the gallantries seemed somewhat jaded, the witticisms a trifle blunt, and the elegance of the men closer to foppishness. After three weeks it became decidedly tedious, and she began to wonder how Kitty weathered it so happily. By the end of a month it was insufferable, and she learned that she was fast gathering a reputation for being tart-tongued and "rather less amusing than her sister."

But Kitty had sparkled enough for both of them, thank heavens. Her pampered, flighty younger sister never failed to be amused, never once neglected to respond at the proper time with her delicious, crystal-tinkling laugh. And Kitty had completed the season triumphantly with a fine offer: a handsome, if rather simpering young man who was sole heir to a viscount's estate in Somerset worth a respectable twelve thousand pounds a year. Not a vast fortune, but generous enough to keep Kitty and her inevitable brood happy for life.

Kitty had earned her beau, and whatever Jamaica thought privately about Timothy Darnley, she could tell there was no question but that he positively doted on her sister. And Kitty? At seventeen she seemed content, even ecstatic about the whole arrangement. It seems incredible, at least to Jamaica, who could no more see herself entering a life of such fatuous domesticity than she could see herself fly. Not, she reflected, that she held anything against marriage; it was simply that she had yet to meet anyone with whom she could entertain the idea. Her aunt had gone to great lengths for them last spring, and from her point of view, Jamaica could see that she was being rather trying, and a certain sense of guilt crept into her thoughts. Chastened, she looked up into her aunt's troubled eyes.

"It's not that I'm less than deeply grateful to you, aunt. I'm truly sorry, but I simply couldn't bring it off." She looked mournfully toward the bibelot that stood close to the duchess's chaise longue. "I don't think I ever could. I simply do not shine in that resplendent company. In fact, I think a second season would be a complete waste of your time and resources."

"Nonsense!"

Jamaica felt her aunt's rising exasperation. Discouraged, she began to wonder if anything was to be gained by pursuing this.

"You lack nothing in deportment or any of the social graces. And as for looks, with a little care and attention, you could be twice the belle that Kitty is. I wish my own girls had your looks. You simply make no effort, Jamie.''

''But I don't want to primp and fuss and simper all the time. I don't find it natural.'' Almost despairing, Jamaica went on doggedly, ''Clearly I don't deserve a splendid match, aunt. Would it not be a distinct relief to you if I were settled in a post and earning my way?''

''But a governess, child! Such a brown-mouse sort of life.'' The duchess was clearly distracted, her mind elsewhere.

''Quite the contrary, Aunt Kate. I would be independent. I adore books and learning and small children, so what could be more fitting? It's a great deal more appealing than settling down with either of the prospects I was offered in London, and far more enticing than a life eked out on my annuity in Paignton.'' She waited, barely drawing breath, for if she was not mistaken, Aunt Kate was softening at last.

But the only response from the duchess was an increasing gravity of expression under the drawn brows.

''Besides,'' she pressed desperately, ''you have Sarah and Charlotte and Melissa to think of. Sarah will be ready next spring, and then two more hard on her heels. I know it's fearful costly, and—'' she hesitated delicately, lowering her head in discomfort at raising the subject ''—I am aware that Camberleigh is shrinking. I know that Uncle George has had to sell off many of the larger farms for lack of tenants during the wars; it does not escape me that these days, not all dukes are made of money. I have no wish to become a burden.''

Jamaica had hit the mark. Outwardly composed, the duchess of Camberleigh sat silently estimating the cost of another season for Jamaica. The girl was definitely becoming a liability, and now she was nineteen. Perhaps it was time for her to know the truth. In light of what the duchess had just learned of the Canwood finances, it was possible that Jamaica was their last asset. At least Oliver Canwood could not borrow against his stepdaughter's marriageability! Kitty had made as good a match as could be expected, but it would hardly redeem her family from Canwood's unerring ineptitude, if that became necessary.

At first she had rejected the idea as too farfetched, but the more she thought on it the more heaven-sent it seemed. That old goat Clare was the perfect solution: rich as Croesus and not one living relative! Until today she had never thought for one moment that her niece would agree. But now, with the girl hell-bent on this piece of sheer whimsy, *now* perhaps she had the bait She looked at her niece blandly.

"There is just a chance that I might look kindly on this fanciful scheme of yours, if you are prepared to be reasonable."

"Then you agree?" Jamaica leaped joyfully from the damask chair and bent to embrace her aunt. "You will really make some inquiries on my behalf? Oh, of course I shall be reasonable, aunt. Oh, I should be so happy!"

"Don't jump to hasty conclusions, Jamie. There is something you should know before we discuss this fantasy any further."

"Yes, aunt?" Jamaica returned to her chair and struggled to assume a docile expression.

"As you know, your stepfather made several investments in the past that I can only describe as spectacularly unsuccessful. In fact, he has quite effectively depleted the fortune your dear father left to your mama when he died."

Jamaica nodded sympathetically, trying not to show her impatience at a recital of facts with which she was all too familiar.

"Last summer he took a rather rash step—rash even for Oliver Canwood. In order to secure a shipping venture, he borrowed heavily against your consols, yours and Kitty's; the market value of the issues absolutely soared after Waterloo. It was apparently more than Oliver could resist. Your mama did very little to dissuade him."

Instead of feeling daunted, Jamaica was sure this added more grist to her mill. "Then it looks very much as if I shall need gainful employment, aunt. I'm surprised that you don't jump at my suggestion."

"I fear the situation is worse than you imagine," the duchess replied reluctantly, "and far beyond remedying with any modest stipend you could earn as a governess. Of course, one hopes for all your sakes that Oliver makes a killing next year, but if his venture fails, there is much more at stake than your annuity from the consols. It will mean Biscay House, as well as your mama's annuity, and whatever trifling assets currently remain. The Canwoods would be ruined, beyond our rescue. You would all be quite run to earth, my dear, unless...."
Here even the stout duchess failed momentarily at the thought of this bright and comely child given over to an old lecher like Clare, but she stiffened her back. She was a de Bowen by marriage and the girl was a de Bowen by birth. One did not shrink from duty, no matter how painful.

"Unless what, Aunt Kate?" Jamaica prompted uneasily.

"Unless you are prepared, out of duty and loyalty, to make an extraordinary match."

"But I've explained, aunt. I lack the grace to bring it off; truly I do," Jamaica said nervously.

"There is one match you would have not the slightest difficulty in bringing off. The only available Englishman I know who is wealthy enough to mend the Canwood fences, more than willing to do so for your sake, and who would marry you at the drop of a glove."

"Really, aunt! Who could there possibly be!"

"Arthur Sterling, marquis of Clare."

"Clare...have we met?"

The duchess nodded, while Jamaica summoned to mind the confusion of aristocrats to whom she had been presented some months ago.

"Clare...Clare...*Clare*!" She gasped as the memory of the man came back to her. "You can't be serious!"

"I am quite serious, child."

"But he's *disgusting*!"

The duchess leaned forward gently and took Jamaica's hand. "He is also very advanced in years, and without heirs; without a single living relative, Jamie! Oliver Canwood could borrow and blunder happily for the rest of his life on such expectations. And your mama need never have another care."

"But Clare!" Jamaica repeated helplessly, trying to summon a picture so intolerable it simply failed to represent itself to the inner eye.

"Now don't get all in a pother about something that most likely will never happen. By next July, if all goes well for your stepfather—and this time it should, Jamie, it really should—you shall all be quite high-steppin' rich again."

"And if it fails to go well...?" Jamaica urged.

"The marquis is a very old man, dear, and not robust. You would surely only have a very few years to endure the marriage. Think of the wealth that would be entirely under your control! Misery is quite endurable when it is silk-lined."

"No! I am prepared to be dutiful, aunt, but duty fails before the idea of such a grotesque union. Absolutely not!"

The duchess shrugged, which her niece took to be a gesture dismissing the loathsome proposal.

"You have laid before me a scheme that is nothing short of outrageous," the duchess said in a tired voice. "You are asking for my blessing and even for the exertion of my considerable influence to bring it about." She shrugged again. "In short, you want me to aid and abet you in perpetrating a scandal. How much do you want this, Jamie?"

"Exceedingly much, aunt. Now, more than ever, when I consider the alternatives."

The duchess fell gloomily silent, a deliberate silence that perplexed Jamaica and at length prompted her to speak up.

"What are you suggesting, aunt?"

"I am suggesting that in order to persuade me to bring about your fondest wish, you must make a promise to me."

"Willingly, aunt. What is it?"

"It is a promise that, after all, you may never be obliged to keep. If your stepfather's gamble succeeds, you will have bamboozled me into something I would never have countenanced under any normal circumstances. So be it. I shall lift my head above the shame. But if, by next July, Oliver fails to secure his loans, you will, without further fuss, leave whatever post I shall have secured for you as governess and marry the marquis of Clare.''

In spite of her plummeting hopes, Jamaica regarded her aunt with an increased respect. The lady was not to be outmaneuvered so easily. "He is quite the richest man in London," she prevaricated. "What leads you to believe that he would have me at the drop of a glove, as you put it, aunt?"

"My dear, I have seen him lick his chops at the mere mention of your name, which, I might as well tell you, he is compelled to drag into every social conversation. If he did not offer for you in the spring, it is only because you are less than half his age, as he is well aware. He has more than once taken your uncle into his confidence."

Jamaica was obliged to suppress a shudder before her gaming instinct came to the rescue. Her father had gambled to his profit on the high seas; his brother, the duke, did quite well at Newmarket. If she was made of de Bowen stuff, she decided, she would not shrink from a sporting chance. She mulled over her aunt's words. *"Whatever post I shall have secured for you as governess...."* So the wily matron was prepared to overcome her sensibilities if need be. It was a good sporting chance.

"You would—you really could find me a post?"

"I'll of course not do it if your mama disapproves."

"If you agree, you know mama will concur. You are the arbiter of society in all of Devon and half of London. Of course mama will agree, if you find it totally *comme il faut*."

The arbiter of Devon society smiled appreciatively at her clever niece, recognizing that she was trying to wheedle her aunt into a one-sided commitment. A last gallant attempt. How very de Bowen!

"It is not *comme il faut*. You know that as well as I do. But it could become so, if I say so." She let out a sad sigh, almost tempted to forget about Clare. Jamaica was such an engaging child. "I suppose it was to be expected that at least one of Henry's children would turn out to be wayward and unconventional."

Jamaica buried her head affectionately in her aunt's alpaca-clad shoulder. "Oh, I'll be so good, aunt. The very soul of propriety. I'll never cause you a moment's embarrassment. You can say I died. I'll work under an assumed name."

"That won't be necessary, young lady. There are de Bowens in gainful employ. Of course, never Camberleigh de Bowens."

"What about my father?" Jamaica asked resourcefully.

"Don't be ridiculous, Jamie. He was a man." The duchess sighed, hardening herself against the girl's melting persuasiveness to deal the final blow. "No, an assumed name won't be necessary; but your word, Jamie, about the marquis. That I must have."

"Must I be bound to it?"

"If your family faces destitution, yes."

"My solemn, irrevocable word?"

"Do not play games with me! I don't do this lightly, child, but out of a duty to protect you and your mama. A de Bowen's word has been trustworthy for twenty-six generations," she reminded soberly.

Jamaica took a deep breath, closed her eyes and plunged. "Very well. If you find me a governess post, you have my word that I will resign it and marry the marquis, should it become necessary."

CATHERINE DE BOWEN, duchess of Camberleigh, stood on the crushed-shell walk the following morning and watched as the phaeton disappeared around the curved carriage sweep, bearing her niece away. Jamaica's going left a mellow sadness in her heart.

The duke was already about his business with the crofters of Apple Creek. He would return before noon and she resolved to tell him then. No point in putting it off. She walked through the glassed-in orangerie and around to the stables, where she bade Matthew, the head groom, ride over to the vicarage to say she would not be able to preside at the good-works breakfast this noon.

She would have to attend the flower-show presentations at five o'clock, she supposed; she was the principal judge of the event. But one duty was all she could manage today. She was decidedly out of sorts.

Armed with pruning shears, basket and canvas gloves, she puttered away the morning in the comfort of the rose garden. There would soon be new varieties from France again, now that the countries were at peace, but Sweet Cornish and Grecian Beauty would always be her favorites, she decided, admiring the creamy perfection of the former and the delicious fragrance of the latter. But today they gave her little consolation; Sweet Cornish only reminded her of Jamaica.

After four sons the duchess had for a time despaired of ever giving birth to a daughter. When her sister-in-law, Emma de Bowen, produced a girl, how she had envied her! Emma was such a helpless, hopeless kind of mother. With Henry away at sea so much, she was forever floundering. It became the domain of the duchess to arrive at the formidable decisions that were quite beyond Emma. *Which nanny—the Wheeler woman or*

*the young girl from Yeovil? Is it the strawberries bother-
ing her or is she cutting teeth? Will it be warm enough at
the picnic to dress her in muslin? Is she too young for a
pony?*

She had never minded; on the contrary, the child had
filled a special place in her heart. Later, when she at last
gave birth to a girl of her own, she discovered to her
chagrin that the infant did not in the least displace
Jamaica in her affections. By that time Jamaica was
three and as precious as an April morning, with her rich
dark hair, glowing creamy complexion and the breezy
charm of her father in perfect miniature. Now full
grown, she was blessed with the features and wand-
slenderness of her mother, and those luminous, incredible eyes, now blue, now green, now both at once!

As the Camberleigh brood increased in number, the
duchess saw less of Jamaica. Regretfully! If only her
mother had taken a firmer hand. What could she not
have done with a charmer like that! She could have
made the most resounding match in all Europe. As it
was, with Henry away most of the time and then dying
so young, the girl had grown *farouche*. Like a wild
flower.

It gave the duchess small consolation that she had
three girls of her own. When it came to grace and beauty, God had forgotten them. They would fare well
enough for husbands, of course; she would see to that
with thorough maternal duty. But to have a Jamaica,
ah, that would have been a special joy!

When Emma remarried after a year of widowhood,
she could hardly blame her; Emma, of all women, needed a man to survive. But to accept Oliver Canwood! Of
all the cherub-faced ninnyhammering nincompoops!
The duchess could positively see the consequences long

before they came about, and for a year or two, she had cut herself off from the Canwoods in disgust. First the copper folly; then a fiasco involving tea and spices from the South Seas; then the stud farm for thorough-breds. The man had an infallible instinct, a positive genius, for losing. And it was to be Jamaica, her heart's delight, who would suffer most from his disastrous efforts. Hence Arthur Sterling, marquis of Clare. There was naught to be done; she could not deprive her daughters in order to support the Can-woods.

As Jamaica had pointed out, Camberleigh had shrunk sadly since the halcyon days when it was a real duchy, stretching for miles south of the Taw and northeast over the downs. The flocks were less than half what they once were because of the reduced pas-tures, and now across the river stood a tannery! What was left had to be preserved at all costs....

Shortly before noon the duchess returned to the house and entered the morning room. The duke, still in his riding boots, sat reading the racing results in the Exeter *Clarion* while he waited for the breakfast bell. He put down the newspaper and rose: a tall, lean, silver-haired man who was aging with physical grace.

"Hallo, m'dear. I thought this was your good-works morning. Didn't expect you at home."

She kissed him on the cheek, then sat without a word on the yellow davenport.

"I say! You look very out of sorts. Anything amiss?"

"George," she sighed, "we have lumpish gels."

The duke colored slightly with irritation. "No need to be so curst blunt about it!"

"I suppose not. I don't give it a thought save when I

see Jamaica. I imagine they will all someday outgrow the ungainly stage,'' she added, unconvinced.

The duke began to pace in front of the davenport worriedly. ''Been meanin' to talk to you about the Canwood girl. Suppose there's no way out. She'll have to have another season. Damned awkward!''

''For heaven's sake, stop calling her the Canwood girl. She's as de Bowen as you are.''

''Well yes, yes. What's it? Jemima?''

''Jamaica, George,'' she said dryly. ''Her name is Jamaica.''

''Confounded stupid name for a girl like that! Told my brother so many a time.'' He stopped pacing and stood for a moment looking down at his wife.

''Been tottin' up the annuals this morning. The harvest just isn't the same with all those tracts gone. The extra season will make quite a pinch. Have to trim things down.'' He knitted his brows tightly. ''Got three of our own, don't y'know?''

The duchess nodded gloomily as her husband continued pacing.

'' 'Struth! Couldn't she walk off with some blade last season? What's the matter with her? Got the looks, don't she?''

''Don't flummox yourself, George. I have resolved the problem.''

''You have?'' The duke brightened. ''Ah, I knew you would! Splendid! Confounded tricky filly, the Canwood girl. Well done!'' He resumed his pacing, but at a more relaxed tempo.

''I am finding her a governess post.''

The duke continued his pacing until the words took hold; then he stopped and turned with a spastic movement of his shoulder.

"A *what*?" His face became slowly scarlet. "Damnation, Kate! The devil you say! Have you clear lost your senses? The girl's me *niece*!"

"Ah, how quickly you remember, George!"

"Damme eyes! Whatever possessed you to commit a blamed folly like that? Governess, indeed! Well, I shan't have it. I shan't!"

"She wanted it," the duchess said, unperturbed.

"She wanted it? One doesn't give a chit of a girl that kind of license because she wanted it! What kind of quick-gab flummery is that? She wanted it! Huh! She wanted it! Huh!" He muttered to himself, jerking like some fantastical animated puppet in near apoplectic amazement.

"George!" she commanded, "if you don't wish to be saddled for life with all three gels, you had better stop that, sit down and listen."

A transformation overcame the duke at his wife's tone of voice. He immediately assumed a deferential air and obediently sat.

Why, she wondered fleetingly, did Henry get the brains and George the title? Was there some divine law of compensation at work? Remembering the contrast between Jamaica and Kitty on the one hand and her own girls on the other, she decided that there was.

"I agreed to let Jamaica have her whim, because in return I was able to extract a very reassuring promise."

"A bargain with the girl?"

"Yes, George. She's agreed to marry Arthur Sterling."

"Good Lord!" He was suitably stunned.

"Yes."

"Then what's she doing governessing? She can't do both!"

"She won't be obliged to marry Arthur unless Canwood fails again. Meanwhile, she can have her little escapade."

He sat silently trying to grasp the subtleties. At length he said, "Ah! Aah! Well then! Yes! The fellow's gone after cotton this time, hasn't he? Very good stuff, cotton. Should make a killing."

"So he should, George, but if anyone can fail in cotton, it will be Oliver."

"Nobody fails in cotton!"

"We are talking about Oliver Canwood, George."

He shook his head. "I see your point. Can't fathom the fellow. Deuced bad luck...everything he touches! His schemes seem sound enough at the start. Don't understand it at all."

"A mysterious gift, George." She looked up with crisp finality. "So you do agree that it was the sensible thing? In return for a year as a governess, she has agreed to marry Arthur if things go the usual way at Biscay House."

"Good Lord, Catherine—Arthur Sterling! You really got her to agree to it! You are a splendid vixen of a woman!"

He took up his newspaper once more and relaxed back into the racing results. But a few moments later he crushed the newspaper suddenly on his knees.

"Catherine! How long did you say before the cotton materializes?"

"Next July, perhaps."

"Next July! What if he don't last?"

"Who, George?"

"Arthur, dammit! He's gout-ridden and ancient and fumble-footed, and he wheezes like a pair of bellows! What if he don't live out the year?"

She sighed. "He's been wheezing for twenty years. One hopes he will wheeze for one more. Still, you're right, George. I suppose one should have an alternative, only there isn't one. No one quite fits the bill like Arthur."

"Or foots the bill either, eh?" He grinned, then turned his head toward the morning room doors in response to a light rap.

"Come in."

Judson entered in his morning uniform. He held out a small silver tray to the duke; it bore an engraved calling card.

"Lord Dorrington, Your Grace. He says that he is staying at Torquay for a few days, and dropped by to wish Your Grace a good day. I was just about to ring the breakfast bell. Are you at home, sir?"

The eyes of the duke and his lady met with a single thought.

CHAPTER TWO

IN SPITE OF THE DREAD POSSIBILITY that descended on her intermittently like a pall, Jamaica resolved to enjoy the journey home. As the splendid matched grays hugged a curve in the coast road, the carriage dipped toward the red clay palisades and she felt her weight sink luxuriously into the yielding velvet upholstery. Aunt Kate's phaeton was most definitely a lady's carriage and no mistake: it was fit for a duchess.

It seemed incredible to her that as a duke's granddaughter, she was part and parcel of the crème de la crème: that featherheaded world of simpering girls, glaring dowagers and self-important dandies.

She glanced at herself in the slim gilt mirror set into the silk quilting above the facing seat. Her face was framed by a starched muslin bonnet tied beneath her chin, the deep moss color matching her dress and echoing her liquid green eyes.

Yes, Aunt Kate was right; if she tried, she could pass for a belle, she supposed. But it was downright tedious to study the silly capricious fashions, and without an abigail, the intricate coiffures were next to impossible. She would far rather spend the time cantering along the sand at low tide, or just curling up with a good book and letting her hair fall where it may.

"Stop being such a bookish stick, Jamie!" Kitty was

forever complaining. "Where's your sense of style? Your sense of romance?"

But quite to the contrary, Jamaica considered herself a romantic down to the very tips of her toes. Her father was nine years gone now, but their special times together, when he was home from the sea, would stay with her always. And such glorious tales he would tell her!

"There's buried treasure there, and in those pirate waters is the most marvelous shade of turquoise, my love. When you make landfall at Jamaica, you can stand on the quarterdeck, peer over the gunwales and look right into an aquamarine sea. And it's just like looking into your eyes. That's why I called you Jamaica. Your eyes are that wonderful hue that you find only in the Carib."

As long as she could remember, she had fed on adventures, first from her father, later from books. The lives of the tall, tanned seafaring men, their desperate battles with the elements, the exotic beauties they loved with a passion that defied race, creed and language...*that* was romance! *That* was style! The London season, on the other hand, was nothing but a marriage mart, a vast exchange of security and convenience. Titles were offered in exchange for plump dowries; ancient names were paired with attractive new fortunes. If a girl, like Jamaica, had only a small annuity, then no matter how splendid her lineage, she had better be well endowed physically and prepared to exert the utmost charm. What pretense! She shuddered, thinking of old Clare. At least there would be no pretense of a love match! She had met him just once at the Fogleby dinner, an evil-eyed old codger who had ogled her bodice all evening. No! It would never come to that. The de Bowens were always lucky in their ventures.

She would put it from her; act and think as she always had. Had she not always promised herself that the only marriage she would make would be a roaring, tempestuous passion? Not for her the careful balancing of debits and credits that passed for love with the Almack set; never! Kitty could have her Mr. Darnley and welcome, but Jamaica's body and soul would remain her own, until someone took them by storm.

And that, she mused as the carriage slowed, was less than likely in a place like Paignton.

She saw from the window that they were approaching the final curve before the fork that led off to Biscay House. This stretch was traveled only by local traffic since the new highway opened. On the left was a formidable drop and barely room for two carriages to pass. For safety the coachman slowed the pair to a walk and held to the center of the road, prepared to give way to an oncoming vehicle if he should hear harness bells approaching from around the bend.

As suddenly as summer lightning, Jamaica felt herself hurled violently over to the far side and pressed against the velvet, as the phaeton swung sickeningly toward the precipice edge, then came to a wrenching, shuddering halt. A team of four horses came at them full tilt, a fearful gallop that their driver could barely restrain; he managed to rein them in and avoid the phaeton by a hairbreadth. She watched agog as a huge post chaise passed her window then slammed into the soft dirt of the palisades. She heard some glass shatter, but the post chaise appeared to be in one piece, although still swaying energetically and pressed hard against the embankment.

Jamaica had no time to panic, but as she stepped down from the phaeton and looked around, she saw its outer wheels gripped in the crumbled dirt just inches away from the sheer drop, and her heart skipped a beat. She made for the black post chaise some paces behind her to inquire after the safety of its passengers. As she approached a door opened. A man leaped from the vehicle and slammed the door forcefully behind him. He was middling tall, rather forbidding, and his face was dark with rage.

"Madam," he shouted, "do you encourage your coachman to drive like a maniac, or is it his natural inclination?"

Maniac! They had almost been driven over the side by his galloping monsters. The gall of the man! She opened her mouth to speak out, but he pressed on.

"In either case, you are grossly at fault. If you cannot control your driver, you have no business being on the road, and your mama should keep you safely at home where you can do less damage."

"How dare you, sir! It was not *my* carriage that came around that curve with a team of four hell-bent racers breathing fire. My driver took every precaution, and he knows this road like the back of his hand."

"Knows it like the back of his hand, does he? Well, he'll get the back of mine if I ever see him again. I know of no law that limits speed, but there is a rule of the road that obliges a vehicle to stay to the left. You were blocking my right-of-way. You are an idiot, ma'am, and I suggest that you and he are well matched." He stabbed the air viciously, pointing at her coachman. "And now, since you are effectively blocking the passage of traffic, I suggest you get back in there and head for your destination. And try to accomplish that without endangering any more unsuspecting travelers, if it's not beyond you."

Jamaica was nearly speechless with rage. She had never been so thoroughly and unjustly abused in her life. But she was grateful to find her tongue again in time for a parting shot.

"You are quite beneath contempt, sir. I suggest you learn the very basis of manners, and some moderation in the speed of your travel before you ever venture abroad again."

But the ringing statement was lost on him. He had turned his back on her as she started to speak, climbed into his carriage and slammed the door.

She walked back to the phaeton and looked up to the high perch. "Let's proceed, Chalmers. I'm sorry you were insulted."

The coachman grinned sympathetically. "Not to worry, ma'am. His lordship's bark is worse than his bite."

"You know him?"

"Oh, yes, ma'am. Not so's I could tell you his name. But he's a gentleman of quality. An occasional house-guest of your uncle."

As Jamaica settled back into the phaeton, she tried to compose herself, wondering why the men she came across were either simpering Milquetoasts or entirely odious, like the boorish stranger and the dreadful marquis of Clare.

In a way, she thought, the encounter had been a good lesson for her. Since she was about to lead a less-sheltered life, it was good to discover that she was not easily browbeaten, and could give as good as she got in an angry exchange. Yes, she decided, the ranting stranger had done her a service. She sincerely hoped she would never see hide nor hair of him again, but if she did, she would be ready for him.

IN THE WHITE GRAVEL DRIVEWAY Jamaica jumped down from the phaeton before it came to rest and waved to her mother, who was sitting under the copper beeches on the south lawn. She turned to her driver. "Would you like to go to the kitchen for some refreshment, Chalmers?"

"Thank you, ma'am, but Her Grace wants us back afore nightfall."

Jamaica leaned on the carriage and removed the light canvas valise that had traveled at her feet. "A glass of cider, then? Surely you won't say no to that?"

The driver smiled broadly, revealing damaged teeth. "Thank you kindly, ma'am. A pot of cider'd be right welcome."

"Good. I'll have one brought out. No, don't get down. I have my valise."

Betty, the scullery maid, burst through the front doors, her mobcap askew, as Jamaica approached the house.

"Welcome back, Miss Jamie." She took the valise from Jamaica's hand and bobbed as she was told to bring out cider for the coachman.

By the time she walked across the lawn to mama, Mrs. Canwood was pink with embarrassment. Jamaica bent to plant a kiss on the flushed cheek beneath the sunbonnet.

"Good day, mama. Is something amiss?"

"The valise!" hissed Mrs. Canwood, with an uneasy look behind her as if the beech trees had treacherous ears. *"The valise."*

"What about the valise?"

"Jamaica, how could you haul out the valise yourself like that? And in front of your Aunt Catherine's coachman! Why didn't you wait for Betty? Why didn't you have the coach drive around to the coach house and have the ostler take care of your trunks?''

"Oh, mama! I hardly had trunks. Just my overnight. And Willie is our gardener as well as ostler. One never knows where to find him. Besides, from what Aunt Kate tells me, I had best get used to not being waited on."

"Jamaica! One does not spread it abroad that one is in straitened circumstances, and particularly not to the servants."

Jamaica gave a sigh of obvious impatience and her mother looked up uneasily from the painted wrought-iron chair. "What did your Aunt Kate tell you?" she asked, plucking at the throat lace of her lavender gown.

"That you have allowed Mr. Canwood to borrow heavily against our consols."

Mrs. Canwood lowered her head. "The consols are in my name, Jamaica. Oliver is my husband, and the law does not—"

"Yes, mama. I know what the law does not. But if you had been properly firm, he would not have gone against your wishes."

"The annuities stop at marriage, and I was sure you would both be settled down by next summer." She brightened. "It is only until next July, dear. Oliver's ship will come to port well before then. After that, your consols will no longer be encumbered and we can pay off the debts against the house. You will, of course, still receive the monthly emoluments."

"Unless Mr. Canwood's investment fails and the consols are forfeit," Jamaica said grimly. "There will be no more monthly emoluments then."

"Did your Aunt Kate suggest that? Never! She has simply been trying to alarm you, Jamie. Your stepfather has invested in cotton, my dear. A cargo from Carolina.

So set your mind at rest. It's as good as gold. Not all his ventures have turned sour, you know. Anyway, I absolutely forbid you to worry about it." She took Jamaica's hand and gave it a motherly pat.

"Now! Tell me how your Aunt Kate is. It was splendid of her to send you home in the phaeton! Did anything else happen at Camberleigh? Did you meet anyone interesting?"

"Everyone is well at Camberleigh, mama." She felt suddenly very weary. "May we talk later? I would like to go to my room." She removed her bonnet. "Is Kitty about?"

"There is no reason for her to know about this," Mrs. Canwood whispered.

"Not a word, mama. I promise. Now, where is Kitty?"

"She's in her room pouting, I'm afraid. Yesterday was not a good day for her."

"What ails her?"

"Mr. Darnley came calling yesterday to take Kitty for a boat ride around Tor Bay. Did you know that Boney is a prisoner aboard the *Bellerophon*? He has requested sanctuary in England and the prince has apparently not decided what to do with him. Meanwhile, the ship is anchored just offshore. They say he walks a turn or two around the deck three times daily for his constitutional. The bay is full of pleasure boats trying to catch a glimpse of him."

"It sounds like a fascinating outing. Why should Kitty be sulking?"

Mrs. Canwood put down her embroidery, exasperated. "Well, you weren't here to chaperone, Jamie! I could hardly let them go alone."

"You could have gone, mama. I should have thought

you would be interested to see the great Emperor-General Bonaparte.''

Mrs. Canwood made a moue. ''You know very well that I cannot abide being on the water. It makes me very ill.''

''I'm sorry, but I didn't know he was expected yesterday.''

''Well that's the very thing of it, Jamie,'' said Mrs. Canwood. ''He was not expected. He came by way of a surprise all the way from Exeter, having heard about the *Bellerophon* and all. So thoughtful of him. It was too bad.''

Bonnet in hand, Jamaica turned toward the house. ''I will try to console her in her great loss!''

''JAMIE!'' Kitty pounced on her sister reproachfully as Jamaica poked her head around Kitty's bedroom door. ''Where have you been?''

''To Aunt Kate's, and you know it.''

Kitty flung herself dramatically onto her bed, her blond curls jiggling. ''Jamie, you absolutely ruined my day yesterday!''

Jamaica grimaced and said nothing.

''Mr. Darnley came around with the most delightful suggestion. He was going to take me sailing and—''

''Yes, I know. Mama has just told me.''

''Ah,'' said Kitty, ''then you know why I am thoroughly cross. Just why you had to go jaunting off to Camberleigh on that very day—and now I'll never in my whole life have an opportunity to see Boney in the flesh. We spent the entire day playing croquet and conversing with mama. It was dreadful. Such a waste!''

''I daresay you and Napoleon Bonaparte will both survive the catastrophe,'' Jamaica commented dryly, "and I'll have you know that my visit to Aunt Kate was not an idle jaunt. I had very serious business to discuss with her."

Kitty rolled her eyes heavenward. "It's rather early to be planning your next season, is it not? The last one has barely finished. Besides—" she carefully arranged the folds of her blue muslin skirt "—if you had not turned so tart and frightened off all the eligibles, there would be no need of another season."

Jamaica picked up Kitty's little boudoir chair and planted it firmly beside the bed, then she sat on the yellow silk seat and leaned forward, nose to nose with Kitty.

"Kitty, stop your wailing and listen. First, I had two offers last spring, which proved I did not frighten away all the eligibles. The fact that I wouldn't be caught dead with either of them is neither here nor there. And second, I did not visit Aunt Kate to discuss another season, and third, there will be no more seasons for me, because I have laid my own plans for the future. Very definite plans."

Kitty widened her china-blue eyes in avid curiosity and waited to hear the rest, but Jamaica rose, bonnet ribbons trailing, and turned with a sweep toward the door.

"If you don't mind, I'm going to wash off the dust of my journey."

Kitty leaped up from the bed and grabbed her escaping sister by the skirts. "Oh, no, you don't, miss! What do you mean, you've laid your own plans? What on earth are you talking about?"

Jamaica whipped her skirts from Kitty's fingers and stood, head high, by the open door. "I shall be taking a post as a governess," she said quietly and left, closing the door rather sharply on a speechless Kitty.

Jamaica fairly ran into her own room and breathed a sigh of relief. It was out, and having told Kitty, she would not have to announce it to mama.

"OH, MAMA, DO SOMETHING!" Kitty wailed. "You simply can't let her do this to us."

Mrs. Canwood looked flustered and helpless; having borne the brunt of Kitty's sporadic outbursts for more than ten days now, she was almost at her wit's end as she looked appealingly at her older daughter.

"You really don't have to do this, Jamie...do you? If marriage is too utterly distasteful to you, well, that happens sometimes. There are some women who simply cannot endure the thought."

"They are called old maids!" Kitty interjected blisteringly.

Mrs. Canwood sighed. "You could always live on your annuity."

Jamaica ground her teeth and stared meaningfully at her mother, who reddened and looked down at her hands.

"I can't think what possessed Aunt Kate to agree," Mrs. Canwood continued, shaking her head slowly.

"She is far more flexible than you suspect, mama," Jamaica replied, wondering how mama would react if she knew about Arthur Sterling.

"What about the duke?" Mrs. Canwood asked querulously.

"As always, he is soft as butter toward anything Aunt Kate has set her mind to."

"But it's you who've set your mind to it," Kitty said accusingly, "not Aunt Kate."

Jamaica shrugged wearily.

"Well, what about Mr. Darnley?" Kitty pursued. "What d'you think he'll say? He didn't bargain on a governess for a sister-in-law."

"If the Duke of Camberleigh can countenance a governess for a niece, I daresay Mr. Darnley will recover from it. I should hope he has more regard for you than that!"

"And what am I to do for a chaperone," she went on, hands on hips, "when he comes calling?"

"Oh, Kitty! In six months you'll be married and no longer need a chaperone. Meanwhile, if I am offered a post, I will not let my usefulness as your chaperone stand in my way. You'll just have to manage."

"Selfish, selfish, selfish!" Kitty wailed, and Jamaica clapped her hands over her ears and ran from the room.

Oliver Canwood peered over his spectacles as Jamaica entered the book room. At fifty-some years his face had the rounded innocence of a sleeping child. Except for his thinning hair one would never have guessed his age.

"Don't overset yourself, Jamie," he crooned, entirely unruffled. "This ado will subside."

Oliver was unlikely to stand in her way; his was not a strong position, and it would never be up to him to yea or nay Jamaica's future. Nevertheless, it soothed her to have him accept her news calmly. Strangely enough she liked him, because he was always content, serene in the face of any setback, and eminently likable.

But to have Oliver on her side did not constitute an ally. It would take Aunt Kate herself, she decided, to smooth the troubled waters before she quite lost her sanity.

In a long letter, she implored the duchess to come to Biscay House.

Before another week was out, mama had received a

soothing missive from Aunt Kate, and Jamaica received a note herself. Aunt Kate would visit her the following Wednesday, and she would not be alone. She would be accompanied by a Mr. and Mrs. John Greville, who were seeking a genteel governess for their three children.

CHAPTER THREE

JOHN GREVILLE HAD A FULL-FACED CORPULENCE that might have bespoken a benign and generous spirit, but the doleful droop of eyes and mouth led Jamaica to suspect that life did not come up to his expectations. Elizabeth Greville, his wife, was dazzling. Her carriage was exquisite; her hair, although undisguisedly graying, was luxuriant, and she was dressed with artful simplicity, elegantly clad in a traveling suit of gray silk. The sum effect of her smart outfit and her admittedly irregular features was greatly pleasing.

Pointedly Aunt Kate took mama into the parlor for a family tête à tête, and Jamaica was left alone with the Grevilles in the book room.

With a flourish Betty placed before them the best Ceylon brew, served in the silver tea service.

Elizabeth Greville broke the awkward silence while Jamaica poured. "We live a very long way from Paignton, Miss de Bowen. Would you not mind being so far from your family?"

"Not in the least, Mrs. Greville."

"Good. Our children are Richard, who is eight, and Sarah, who is nine. They have been virtually at play since our governess resigned in June. I'm afraid she left them a very small legacy of learning. If Richard is to enter Winchester College when he is nine, you would have your work cut out for you."

Jamaica looked up quickly. "I understood from my aunt that you have three children. Was she mistaken?"

Mrs. Greville glanced briefly at her husband. "There are three children in our household, yes. The third child, Caroline, belongs to my husband's brother. She has just turned five."

"My brother," Mr. Greville cut in, "is a widower. For three years he served under Wellington in the wars and his daughter lived with us. When he returned to his estates, we discussed the child's future, and he deemed it best for the child to remain with us."

"She is not an easy child," Mrs. Greville said, breaking the slightly strained silence that followed, "having spent her tender years without a mother and—virtually—without a father, too. She will attend lessons along with Sarah and Richard, and would be entirely in your charge."

Jamaica raised her eyebrows questioningly. As a governess she had not expected quite so young a charge; she would have thought a nanny far more appropriate than a governess.

Mrs. Greville sensed her question. "Although, as I say, she is not an easy child, you will find her clever, Miss de Bowen, and quick to learn. I believe she is in need of cherishing."

Jamaica said nothing, but the last statement puzzled her. She would have guessed the child was pampered, but in need of cherishing?

"Her father is not an affectionate man," Mrs. Greville added.

"There is no love lost between them," Mr. Greville said bluntly. "But enough of Caroline. Tell us about yourself, Miss de Bowen. Your aunt says you're quite a scholar. How did you come to be so?"

Jamaica was vexed at the change of topic; more questions had been raised than answered, but out of courtesy, she responded to his question.

"I would hardly describe myself as a scholar, Mr. Greville. I learned to read early because I was anxious to learn about my father's voyages and to follow his maps."

"Ah! A seafarer, was he not?"

"Yes, sir, and very knowledgeable. He recognized in me a similar curiosity to his own and so shared his travel observations."

Jamaica rose and moved to the carved oak globe that stood in the bow window. "Before every voyage he would draw me a map until I learned to draw them myself from memory."

The Grevilles put down their teacups and joined her by the window to examine the unusual, intricate carving on the curved surfaces. The bas-relief distinguishing land masses from ocean was quite magnificent.

"Each time he sailed I would read everything I could find—" she twirled the globe lovingly as she spoke "—about the Straits of Magellan, Cape Horn, the West Indies, the Barbary Coast, the South China Seas. ..." Jamaica gestured with pride at the three book-lined walls. "My grandfather left his library to my father, my uncle having little taste for reading. We have added to it over the years."

Jamaica returned to her chair and continued as she refilled the teacups. "I confess I became a glutton for reading: fact and fiction, history, geography and myth. I am also schooled in Latin, French and German, and I know a little Italian."

"You sound impressively learned, Miss de Bowen," Mrs. Greville said with open admiration. "Bravo for you!"

"Very commendable," Mr. Greville said, "but I was thinking more of simply teaching the children to read well and to improve their penmanship. Perhaps you might find that a trifle dull?"

"Quite the contrary, Mr. Greville. I should be charmed to start with the very humblest fundamentals. To inspire young minds to search for knowledge would be a privilege."

"And computation? How is your arithmetic?"

"Fie, John!" Mrs. Greville said, blushing. "I'm sure you underestimate the lady."

"No, no, Mrs. Greville," Jamaica smiled, "it is a fitting question. The children will, of course, need computation, and I believe I can adequately teach them their multiplications and long division, although I did not excel in mathematics at Miss Crawford's School for Girls."

"Well, that will more than see Richard into Winchester," Greville said. "Of course, Sarah won't ever need more than that."

"I also play the pianoforte—poorly, but well enough to teach the fundamentals—and I sketch and watercolor and I will explain the important affairs of the day to the children when I read the newspaper and I would be quite delighted if you would consider me suitable for the post," Jamaica poured out in one breath.

Mrs. Greville noncommittally steered the conversation into more general areas and they chatted informally, exchanging insignificant information. Jamaica observed a courtesy extended toward her that bordered on deference, at least a politesse that was surely not called for from an employer. It was her aunt's rank, she decided uneasily, concerned lest it might make the Grevilles hesitant to take her on as hired help.

At length Mrs. Greville asked to speak again with Aunt Kate.

"Of course," Jamaica replied. "I will ask her to join you here." She waited discreetly in the parlor while her aunt conferred mysteriously with the Grevilles. Mama, she noted, had been much comforted by Aunt Kate's visit. In fact, she now seemed to regard the affair as a jaunty adventure. Although aware of mama's deep respect for Aunt Kate, Jamaica was nevertheless surprised at the former's suddenly high spirits.

"Well," Mrs. Canwood had said gaily, "I suppose we'll have to put together a rather modest new wardrobe for you. Dark browns, grays and navy blues, I should think. Bombazine, of course."

"Bombazine! That is for mourning, mama."

"And for governessing, too, no doubt, dear," her mother had replied, teasing gently.

Jamaica was called back into the book room in precisely fifteen minutes.

"We should like to offer you the post, Miss de Bowen. At one hundred pounds a year," Mr. Greville said formally. "Rather more than is usual, but then you are more than usually accomplished. You shall have a bedroom and sitting room of your own, Sunday afternoons completely free, and you shall arrange a program of lessons appropriate to the family schedule of meals and so forth. You shall breakfast with the children and dine with us, unless we are entertaining, in which case you shall have a tray brought to your room. . . ."

While Mr. Greville continued to describe the conditions of her employment, Jamaica's head spun, and she hardly heard him. One hundred pounds! It was close to two pounds a week! She knew that a miner got at most thirteen shillings a week—almost a quarter of the amount—and from that he had to feed and shelter a family, too. She had no idea a governess was paid so much. Why, it was almost as much as her annuity! The idea of earning four times what a man could earn, and entirely of her own efforts, was suddenly intoxicating.

She realized Mr. Greville had finished speaking. "I accept with pleasure," she said quickly.

"Splendid!" Mrs. Greville said, and gave her a quick hug. "John and I are passing the month in Torquay. Can you be prepared to travel with us when we leave at the beginning of September?"

KITTY DID NOT SPEAK TO HER for almost a week, but Jamaica hardly noticed. She was filled with purpose and plagued with curiosity. How she would have liked a private talk with Aunt Kate before she left Biscay House, but there was no chance. She ached to know more about the Grevilles.

Mama proved to be a disappointing source of information. "All I know is that your aunt knew Mr. Greville's parents, the earl and countess of Dorrington, both deceased. As far as I can tell, it's a respectable family."

Jamaica hoped to broach her aunt on the subject before she left for her post in three weeks' time, but the duchess wrote informing them that she had gone with the girls to her brother in Somerset. She wished Jamaica good fortune in her post, and Jamaica knew she would have to satisfy herself with the meager facts she had and what she would eventually discover for herself living with the Grevilles.

Living with the Grevilles. It had an almost frightening sound. She had a fleeting vision of spending the rest of her life in dark blue bombazine, and although she had never cared the least for flounces, she felt suddenly unaccountably deprived. Would there be no more jaunts to Camberleigh, no picnics, no riding on the sands? Was she not to have callers or entertain friends again? Would she shrivel into a mousy old maid? Had her aunt arranged for her such a dismal environment that she would fly uncomplaining into old Sterling's arms, should it be required of her? Perish the thought!

She threw her nervous energies into poring over every item of clothing she possessed. She owned nothing in bombazine. She examined her brilliantine, a much finer material with its blend of best cotton and alpaca—perhaps too fine for a governess? Surely there were no hard-and-fast rules? With relief she recalled that she was to dine with her employers when they were not entertaining. Of course! Her muslins and sarcenets would be quite appropriate.

"I declare," said Mrs. Canwood, who had offered very little help in the decision, "now you're to be a governess, you are more fashion conscious than you've been in nineteen years; more than Kitty, I do declare!"

"I just want to be entirely fitting, mama!"

KITTY MADE HER PEACE one evening after mama had retired and Oliver was away. In a mood of utter generosity, which was one of her redeeming features, she hugged Jamaica.

"I've been so beastly, Jamie! Will you ever forgive me?"

"You are my only sister, Kitty! It is already forgotten."

"I shall miss you so, Jamie. That's why I fought it so much, but I know it's what you want. Please be happy; I hope so very much you'll be happy."

She knew she would miss Kitty, too; for all her flighty, narcissistic ways, Kitty was very precious to her. A gloom descended on Jamaica that she was hard put to dispel. It did not help when a few days later a carter came to collect her trunks and take them on ahead.

Alone in her room one morning, Jamaica sadly fingered the filmy dress that she had worn as a tea gown in London last spring. She had considered it too coquettish to take with her to the Grevilles. Looking at its gossamer white tissue floating over the creamy muslin underdress, she felt it was the kind of thing she would never wear again. It had been a wrench putting her trunks into the carter's hands, like a point of no return. Just eight days of freedom left....

On an impulse she took the cream-colored London dress from her garderobe, and removing her morning gown, she stepped into it. She dressed her hair with unusual care, brushing it until it shone, then coiling it into a thick lustrous chignon. She pulled some wispy curls toward her forehead and temples after the present fashion. This, she decided, was how she would say farewell to the West Country. She had chosen the morning well, for the gig was at her disposal. Mr. Canwood was at the Exeter horse fair with his crony, Peter Frimton, and would not be back for several days. Mama was fussing over the refreshments to be served at the piquet tea this afternoon for the card-playing ladies of Paignton, and Kitty was closeted in her room with a letter from Mr. Darnley and a set of sketches of her wedding gown that had arrived by post just yesterday. They would no doubt keep her busy all day.

Not wishing to spoil her fragile dress, she pulled Willie away from his weeding around the delphiniums and had him harness the mare. Apple was getting on in years, but this morning, like Jamaica, she could sniff the brisk hint of autumn in the air and was raring to go.

Jamaica set off in the gig, making toward the coast road. There was rather more traffic than she expected, and remembering the close shave in Aunt Kate's phaeton, she decided to branch off the highway, skirt the village of Paignton and drive through Elm Wood on to the green hills that lay beyond. The path was smooth for the first mile or so, because this was the access to the main thoroughfare leading into Newton Abbot.

Apple trotted obediently up the smooth cobbles, past the Golden Gosling Inn and on to the country road where cows grazed on either side and huge horse chestnuts shaded the way. Apple slowed down, laboring slightly as they climbed out of Elm Wood, and Jamaica knew that from the far side of the wood, after the road ascended for half a mile, one could turn around and look over the tops of the trees right across to the sea. As the climb subsided into the level stretch, she turned and caught her breath. It was the season of turning leaves, and as the sun caught the color, it changed to pale gold, the last of the morning's dew glistening like diamonds. And there, clear across Elmwood, was the restless, silvered sea.

"Look due East from here, Jamie," her father had said. *"Like this. If you sail from here in a straight line, you'll make landfall at St. Quentin. Two days' sailing in a fair breeze. And when you land, if you stay in the same direction, it's just a short march to Crécy, where Edward, the Black Prince, vanquished a hundred thousand Frenchmen led by their king. That was almost five hundred years ago, and he was a lad of sixteen."*

There would be no vistas to match this at the Grevilles', nor memories. She let her eyes linger lovingly on the beautiful sight.

Jamaica turned quickly back in her seat when she felt a jolt and heard Apple's hooves miss a beat. Then, after a dreadful grinding sound, the gig dipped over to one side and came to rest, one wheel off and rolling into the ditch. Jamaica slid from the seat to the ground, picked herself up, and dusted off her skirts.

"There, there, Apple. It's all right. Not your fault." She soothed the mare's withers with her hands as she considered her alternatives. She could leave Apple tethered to a tree and walk down to the Golden Gosling—it was not more than two miles and downhill all the way— or she could walk Apple down with her, which would be somewhat slower. The only thing she couldn't do, in this dress, was ride Apple bareback down the hill. She decided there were too many horse thieves in these parts to leave the mare unattended, and she began to unbuckle the harness. The second buckle was stubborn; the harness straps had been wrenched in the accident, and she stood struggling with it. After a few moments she stopped, carefully examining the harness to see if there was another way to detach Apple from the shafts.

"Good morning, ma'am. May I be of help?"

The deep voice behind her on the deserted road made her jump. She turned around to confront quite the most handsome man she had ever laid eyes on. She knew instantly he was a seaman. The sun-washed blue eyes were circled by premature wrinkles that came from squinting at the horizon, the dark tan that made his teeth so white was pure sea wind and sky, and the kind of sun that didn't shine off the coast of Devon. The soft brown hair was sun-bleached, too. He was wearing light nankeens, tucked leanly into well-polished hessian boots. His fine lawn shirt was deeply open across the chest, in the fashion Lord Byron had made the rage. His coat was flung casually over one broad shoulder, and he was loosely holding the bridle of a chestnut stallion. The overall effect, with the sun dappling the broad expanse of his shirt and the leaves rippling overhead, was so overpowering that Jamaica stood and gaped. Recovering herself and feeling idiotic, she could think of nothing to say but "Oh!"

"Please forgive me. I startled you."

"You did, indeed," said Jamaica, pleased to have a valid excuse to cover her lapse.

He bowed elegantly. "Andrew MacFarland, ma'am, petty officer aboard the *York Minster* at Tor Bay. And anxious to be of service."

Jamaica nodded briefly. "Jamaica de Bowen, sir. And I thank you kindly. I was about to untether my mare here and walk down with her to the inn."

"Well, you shan't walk, Miss de Bowen," he said, taking the harness from Jamaica's hands and extracting the mare with ease. "You shall have my trusty stallion here and ride in the saddle. I'll lead your mare and accompany you."

Jamaica blushed and was rather surprised at herself. "I'm afraid, Mr. MacFarland, that I won't be able to ride; I'm not dressed for it. But I would much appreciate the company down to the inn."

He glanced down to her feet. "Well, you certainly can't walk this dusty road. You'll ruin your pretty silk slippers!"

She smiled, feeling very foolish. How absurdly dressed she was for a country drive! "No great tragedy, Mr. MacFarland, I'll—"

Suddenly his arms were around her waist and she was lifted high onto the saddle as if she weighed no more than a cloth doll. He set her down gently, sideways.

Jamaica was speechless.

"Just an old hack from the inn; not a sidesaddle, I'm afraid. I didn't anticipate a damsel in distress. No, don't worry," he said gaily as she tried to protest, "I'll hold you. You won't slide."

And hold her he did! Jamaica was stunned at his audacity, as he handed her the stallion's reins and led Apple away from the gig and down the path, all in one fluid movement.

"Your gig came a cropper, I see. Was it a stone? A tree root? I'd fix it myself, but I see the axle's snapped. We're going to have to find a wheelwright. We shall inquire at the inn."

"There's a wheelwright in the village, Mr. MacFarland," she said, very aware that her skirts were raised and her stockinged legs were showing almost to the knee. *If I insist on getting down from this undignified position,* she thought, *I'll have to jump down more or less into his arms.* She was scarlet to the roots of her hair, but he smiled down gaily, not seeming to notice her discomfort.

"I'm sorry if this isn't quite *comme il faut*, Miss de Bowen," he said at last, with the charming air of a penitent schoolboy, "but it does at least save your slippers and give me an excuse to attend you quite closely." His arm tightened around her waist.

"Really, Mr. MacFarland! We have hardly been introduced!"

"I know. I can hardly believe my good fortune." His smile was devastating. "Please not to worry. You are quite safe with me, and we shall be at the inn very soon. Too soon, for me."

Jamaica thought it safest to say nothing, and for the rest of the journey, he behaved well enough. At one point where the descent was steepest, Jamaica felt herself slip from the saddle literally into his arms. He apologized, set her back on the horse and refrained from any ungentlemanly insinuations, for which she was grateful. The sensation had not been entirely unpleasant, she noted.

At the Golden Gosling he would hear of nothing but that Jamaica sit comfortably in the guests' parlor with a cool drink. He left while she composed herself and returned in a few minutes.

"I've ordered a hackney to take us to Fetterman's, Miss de Bowen, but it won't be available for more than an hour. As far as I'm concerned, that's splendid news. I'm exceedingly hungry and the food is quite good here. Will you do me the honor of joining me for breakfast?"

If he hadn't been quite so handsome, she thought, it would be easier to remember propriety. But he stood and bowed and held out his arm, and looked so utterly the tall, tanned, seafaring man, that she answered, "With pleasure, Mr. MacFarland," hardly believing her ears.

"NOW I SHALL TAKE YOU HOME," he announced as they left Fetterman's barn. Jamaica realized that he had entirely taken over once again, arranging for the wheelwright's cart to pick up the gig and bring it back to the village for repairs, arranging for Apple to be stabled overnight at the inn—enough was enough, she decided.

"You have troubled yourself more than sufficiently already," she protested. "I can get home quite safely from the village, Mr. MacFarland."

"Please give the driver directions. I insist." He smiled, unperturbed, and Jamaica found herself meekly instructing the hackie to Biscay House.

"An interesting name, Biscay House," he remarked, settling back into the seat with her. "Is there a story attached to that?"

· My father was once master of a freighter named *The Bay of Biscay*."

"A sea-captain's daughter!" he exclaimed with delight. "Of course; I should have known when you introduced yourself. Who but a sailing man would name his daughter Jamaica!"

He gazed at her with an open ardor she found rather embarrassing in the close quarters of the carriage. "It was your eyes, of course. The color of the waters around that island."

"How very clever of you, Mr. MacFarland." Jamaica felt uncomfortably warm.

After explanations, Mr. MacFarland was greeted at Biscay House with effusion from mama, Kitty and the card-playing ladies.

Jamaica was thoroughly relieved when he declined to stay for dinner because he was expected back aboard the *York Minster* before eight bells.

"Eight bells!" mama giggled. "Oh, Mr. MacFarland, I have not heard that expression for a very long time."

As she walked Mr. MacFarland back to the waiting hackney, Jamaica decided that it had been a pleasant interlude, nothing more. He was dangerously charming, but a seafaring man rarely settled down in his youth; besides, it was evident that if he wished he could catch one of the fairest prizes of the London season, and if he paid court to her he would be no more than trifling. She had already charted her course, she reminded herself.

She was therefore a little startled when he turned, before entering the hackney, and with no warning at all, asked, "Are you spoken for, Miss de Bowen?"

"Yes, Mr. MacFarland," she replied, after the briefest pause.

"Of course. How could I doubt it?" His mouth drooped in a comical lampoon of despair. "Who is the dastardly lucky fellow?"

"Not a fellow, Mr. MacFarland; a family. I have decided that I am not ready for marriage, and perhaps will never be. I leave for London in eight days to take up a governess post."

If this raised any questions in his mind, he did not voice them or register surprise, but stood gazing intently into her eyes.

He took her hand and grazed it lightly with his lips. "You shall be the most charming governess in all London."

"I rather doubt it, sir." She felt uncomfortably warm once more. "I shall at any rate be a governess in London."

"Shall you have gentlemen callers?"

She was taken aback. "I have not inquired of my employers if it is permissible."

"You shall have one, at all events. Who is to be your employer?"

"The Grevilles of Kensington."

"We leave for Plymouth on the tide. But before November I shall be at liberty. And in London, never doubt it, Jamie."

He turned, calling, "To the port, driver!" and was gone before his impudence had fully registered.

CHAPTER FOUR

As she prepared to leave Biscay House, Jamaica found herself giving much thought to the provocative Mr. MacFarland. Would he actually call on her at her place of employment? He was certainly intrepid enough to do so, but November was more than two months off; she fancied that he was light-minded enough to have forgotten her completely by then. She recalled the soft Scottish burr in his speech. Edinburgh, perhaps. But his diction was upper-class, with the perfect vowels of Harrow school. Yes, there was no doubt he was a gentleman, with a gentleman's schooling—which, of course, did not preclude him from being a scoundrel.

She became thoroughly vexed with herself and pushed the shallow thoughts away, but found them returning as she prepared for the journey to Kensington. It was a relief when at last the day came and, tearful goodbyes over, she was on her way with the Grevilles.

They made the journey not in a family carriage but by Fenniman's Express, a hackney service that plied between Tor Bay and Cheapside. With fresh horses at every stage, the two hundred miles were covered in a scant three days; hard-riding, tedious days, to be sure, but Mrs. Greville was now anxious to see her children, awaiting them in Kensington.

Jamaica quickly discovered that John Greville was no great conversationalist, but Elizabeth, with unusually facile wit and charm, eased the long rumbling hours with amusing discourses. Increasingly, Jamaica warmed to Mrs. Greville and decided that whatever lay before her, that lady's charm would make her duties pleasant.

"Courage, Miss de Bowen," Mrs. Greville said smiling, on the second-night stop.

They were lodged at The Fighting Cocks in Guilford. After dinner at the inn, Mr. Greville joined a gaming table in the saloon, and the two women lingered awhile in the small solarium to admire the view of the moonlit gardens outside.

"By tomorrow evening we shall be home; we shall do our very best to make it feel like home to you. You shall have a hot bath if it's not too late, and your clothes and private things will be waiting for you in your rooms."

"It will be much appreciated, Mrs. Greville, and I so look forward to meeting the children."

Mrs. Greville gave a humorous smile. "I have warned you, have I not, that Richard and Sarah are thoroughly rambunctious and have no doubt been dreadfully spoiled over the summer by my father."

"You did mention it, but I am not overly apprehensive."

"Well, I don't think I can stress it too much!" Her smile faded as she drew her perfect brows together in concern. "I do hope Lord Dorrington is not being too hasty in believing that Caroline has no more need of a nanny. It does seem to me that you may be serving double-duty for a while, even if she is a self-sufficient little thing. She's quite precocious, but she's only five."

"Don't concern yourself too much, Mrs. Greville. Small children generally take to me, and I to them." Jamaica was not as confident as her words implied. In fact, she had very little experience of small children, but she found herself anxious to reassure Mrs. Greville.

"You shall help me convert the nursery into a proper schoolroom. Caroline's little cot is still there; we shall have to open the west wing and do one of the rooms for her. It's part of the house we have never used. The rooms adjacent to the nursery were nanny's. They shall be yours now. It's quite an old barn of a place, as you shall see."

They sat for a while watching the moon silvering the wet grass of the lawns beyond the tall windows.

"Miss de Bowen," Mrs. Greville said suddenly, "we do not always agree with Lord Dorrington's ideas on raising Caroline. We find him overly severe toward her, but she is his child, and there are certain mitigating circumstances." Her wide eyes became very candid and she lowered her voice slightly. "Of course, Charles—Lord Dorrington—is providing the wherewithal for us to live the way we do."

Jamaica was acutely embarrassed at this revelation. She had already gathered that the shadow of Lord Dorrington hung heavily on this family. "Well," she murmured soothingly, "firstborns can grow up to be rather trying to their younger brethren."

There was an awkward silence, which Jamaica felt compelled to fill. "My father was a second son," she offered, "and I have felt the sting of it myself from time to time. My aunt is quite the—"

"My husband is not a second son," Mrs. Greville said with quiet deliberation. "He is the elder of the two. He was disinherited for marrying me."

As she felt her color rise, Jamaica fixed her eyes on the towering oak trees that shadowed the farthest extremity of the lawn, glad that there was no chandelier and that the solarium was dimly lit. "I'm so sorry, ma'am. I did not mean to pry."

Mrs. Greville laid a gentle hand on her arm. "Please! You did not pry. I am telling you freely what is a rather well-known fact in London. I am—or was—an actress, Miss de Bowen. On the London stage. I am a Norfolk gamekeeper's daughter. I have never concealed that fact, nor do I intend to start now." She leaned back in her window seat, quite at ease. "If you have mistaken me for a lady of quality, it is only because I am an accomplished actress. It is simply a masquerade."

"No, Mrs. Greville! No masquerade! You are the very soul of grace and refinement. To me, that defines a lady of quality."

The lady gave a self-deprecating little shrug. "Be that as it may, Miss de Bowen, at least there shall be no pretense between us. The truth is that when John married me, in open defiance of his father's threats, he was immediately cut off without a penny. I was obliged to continue plying my art in the provinces, or we would have lived like paupers. It was not until my father-in-law died and Charles came into the earldom that we were able to live comfortably. Charles settled the Kensington house on us, and a handsome annuity. My brother-in-law has always been most magnanimous, without any obligation."

"Then he has a more generous spirit than his father," Jamaica said. "It is difficult for me to understand why he cannot display a similar generosity of feeling toward his daughter."

"Caroline's mother died just months after giving birth."

"And he blames Caroline for it?" Jamaica was incredulous. But she could see Mrs. Greville was no longer at ease, and was shaking her head as if she wished to dismiss the subject.

"Would you like a pot of tea?" she asked sweetly.

Jamaica took the hint that the discussion had gone far enough. "Indeed I would, Mrs. Greville, and then, if you would excuse me, I think I should like to retire. We shall need to be up by six o'clock, I believe."

GREVILLE HOUSE was a rambling ivy-covered manor, about fifty years old. It was one of a small cluster of gracious houses whose mullioned windows faced the royal gardens of Kensington, now open to the public, and the serene wide lake known as the Serpentine. Kensington had retained the green aspect of a country village, but its inhabitants referred to it now as London, since one could take a brisk walk past the Serpentine into Hyde Park, and find oneself on the Bayswater Road in one direction and Piccadilly in the other.

Last night they had arrived too late to see the children. Jamaica now awaited a morning rendezvous with Mrs. Greville.

"I will fetch you a little before eight o'clock," Mrs. Pruett, the housekeeper had told her last night after showing Jamaica to her rooms. "Mrs. Greville will see you in the morning room and introduce you to the children."

In anticipation Jamaica had woken too early, and she slipped out to view the house and its environs in daylight. Now, as she hurried, a little uncertain, back to her sitting room, she realized how large and confusing the house was, and why the housekeeper was needed to lead her to the morning room.

"Ah, Miss de Bowen! I hope you slept well. I should like you to meet Richard, Sarah and Caroline."

"Good morning, Mrs. Greville. How do you do, children." Jamaica held out her hand to each of the older children.

Sarah was a round-faced version of her mother, with reddish brown curls and wide eyes. Richard was thin, coltish and very fidgety.

Caroline, the smallest, was partially hidden behind Mrs. Greville's skirts, and when her head peeked out from irresistible curiosity, Jamaica saw the pale frightened face of a baby, still soft and round.

"Come on, Carrie," Mrs. Greville said, gently tugging the reluctant child clear of her skirts. "What do you say to Miss de Bowen? She's come a long way to meet you."

Slowly Caroline came forward. Her enormous gray eyes were soulful, and the sherry-colored hair was pulled rather severely back from her face. It was the face of a sad little cherub seeking love, Jamaica thought, and then she noticed the startling severity of the child's dress under the soft little chin. Caroline wore an overly large tunic made of dark gray bombazine. There was not even a light collar or cuffs to relieve the dreariness of it. Next to the pink muslin and white silk trim of her cousin Sarah's dress, it was grotesque.

She knelt down and took Caroline's hand. "I'm so happy to meet you, Carrie. May I call you that, too? I hope we shall be friends. I am sorely in need of a friend."

At last Caroline lifted her head after a bobbed curtsy. "How do you do, Miss de Bowen."

"Now, let's all sit down and have our chocolate," Mrs. Greville said with a sigh of relief.

It was a full day—becoming acquainted with the children, touring the house with Mrs. Greville, and making plans for the immediate remodeling of the nursery and the removal of Caroline's bedroom to the west wing. It was not until after dinner that night, when the children were in bed, that Jamaica was able to address Mrs. Greville on the subject of Caroline's appalling clothes.

Mrs. Greville responded with a sad little smile. "I was wondering when you would ask. Dreadful, is it not? A notion of Lord Dorrington's."

"But she looks like an orphan in a poorhouse! Surely he does not wish his own daughter to be dressed so!"

"Yes, it is hard to believe, and of course it distresses me, too. While he was away at the wars, I dressed her appropriately—like Sarah. There was quite a scene when he returned. It was the first time he had seen her out of infant wrappers. He insists that I was turning her into a light-skirt."

"A light-skirt!" Jamaica could not help laughing.

"Truly! He stormed out of here one day and returned with a box of those dreadful things, and removed all her pretty dresses." Mrs. Greville bit her lower lip. "It has been a bone of contention between us all year. He has forbidden me to buy her clothes. For Carrie's sake, I have gone along with it."

"For Carrie's sake?"

"Miss de Bowen, she is a very sensitive child, as you shall soon learn, sensitive to a quarrelsome atmosphere. She is so distressed by conflict that I have decided it is best to try to keep the peace."

Jamaica found this impossible to accept. "Surely," she pressed on, "with Sarah in her pretty muslins, it is too cruel?"

Mrs. Greville sighed wearily. "My hands are tied, in effect. We have certain obligations to my brother-in-law."

Jamaica sat thinking for a few moments, then she looked up at her employer. "Do you have any of Sarah's dresses—old ones that she has outgrown?"

"I have all of them—darling little things. But it won't work, Miss de Bowen."

"But surely—I sew a little; they could be made to fit Caroline?"

"I don't doubt it, but—" Mrs. Greville shook her head.

"But your promise not to buy her clothes shall not be broken, and she will at least look as if she belongs here."

Hearing the note of urgent pleading in Jamaica's voice, Mrs. Greville wavered. "I promise you, Lord Dorrington would be furious. . . ." She paused, weighing the situation.

"Since I have charge of Caroline, I shall be happy to take full responsibility for the decision, and to defend it to Lord Dorrington. I am sure he can be made to see the reasonableness of dressing the child in a manner that makes her feel comfortable with her cousins."

Mrs. Greville smiled at her confidence. "I have my doubts, but since you feel so strongly, for decency's sake, let's try by all means. Perhaps he has grown less morbid over the summer," she said hopefully, then grinned brightly at Jamaica.

"We shall burn the hateful bombazine."

"That," Jamaica responded, "would be a singular pleasure."

WITHIN A DAY Caroline was transformed into a pastel princess in muslins, silks and velveteens. Tiny lockets, rings and bracelets appeared from Mrs. Greville's mementos; the child's rich hair was brushed long and silky and tied with ribbons that matched each dress in her new wardrobe.

By the end of the week the nursery was refurnished with a writing desk for Jamaica, three smaller desks for the children, an easel and a chalkboard. Supplies of paper and pens, and a small slate for each of the children, completed the school equipment.

Caroline's nursery cot was replaced by a four-poster bed in a huge room of the west wing. Mrs. Greville assigned a chambermaid to take care of Caroline's clothes and hair, but it was Jamaica, out of choice, who tucked her into bed each night.

On Caroline's first night in the deserted west wing, Jamaica was concerned for the child's spirits. Listening outside the room, she heard whimpers. She entered to find the child sucking her thumb and curled up under the blankets in a tight frightened ball.

"It's me, Carrie," she called out, "Miss Jamie. Can I come in?"

"Y-yes, Miss Jamie," the child replied, trying hard to disguise her sobs.

"Would you like me to stay until you go to sleep?"

"I'd like you to stay with me all night, miss, like nanny did." Caroline was crying openly now.

"She did?"

"Yes, Miss Jamie. In a bed so close to mine that I could reach out my hand and touch it."

Jamaica put her arms tightly around the child, feeling a decided tug on her heartstrings. "I think this bed is big enough for both of us, don't you?"

It became a habit. Caroline would fall asleep content, knowing that later that night, Jamaica would climb into the four-poster beside her.

Caroline quickly became Jamaica's devoted slave,

studying her lessons avidly and begging to fetch and carry for her. In schoolwork the child was a source of amazement. Jamaica had been prepared with a separate course of instruction for her that was half play, half work. But the child had begged to follow the same lessons as her older cousins. Whether it was from a natural brilliance or a feverish determination to earn her approval, Jamaica could not decide, but Caroline kept apace with Richard and Sarah—and with apparent ease.

The autumn days at Greville House fell into an established pattern. Lessons were mornings from half-past eight until lunchtime, with two short breaks. In the afternoon there were walks or rides in the gardens, followed by a short rest. Their evening meal was at five o'clock. Then they would play quietly or work at their hobbies until bedtime. Shortly before the adult dinnertime, they would go downstairs to wish mama and papa good-night.

As the children handed her their exercises one morning, Jamaica was surprised to realize that three weeks had passed. She was, she decided, a success. Richard and Sarah were rambunctious only in the park now. Study progress was evident and Caroline had lost all her nervous shyness. She smiled as she glanced at Richard's paper. His execrable spelling was improving at last.

She looked up at the expectant faces. "I think I smell beef and kidney pie. You may remove your smocks now, children."

They scrambled up from their desks eagerly.

"Wash the ink from your hands first. And Sarah, take Caroline to the washbasin and see that she gets all the ink off her fingers this time before she touches her muslin." She watched them run off to the far end of the room and disappear behind the screen that partitioned off the utility area where a washbasin stood, storage cupboards and hooks to hang up their smocks. Then she returned her concentration once more to the children's papers.

Moments later she heard a commotion. She looked up to see a man emerging from behind the screen. He was holding an intimidated Caroline by the scruff of the neck while he scolded her roughly.

As Jamaica rose from her chair and rushed forward, Caroline pulled away from the man and ran to her. Jamaica clasped the child protectively, then looked up at the intruder with a sudden shock of recognition. It was the dreadful man whose post chaise had almost driven her over a cliff in Paignton! The memory of the outrage jolted her into instant action.

"Leave this room immediately! How dare you lay a finger on this child!" she shouted.

The intruder raised an eyebrow, then a slow sardonic smile of recognition spread over his features. "Bless my soul! The lurking peril of the Devonshire highways. The fiend of the phaeton in the flesh!" Feet planted wide, arms folded, he eyed her with insufferable arrogance. "What the devil are you doing here?"

Caroline scrambled down from Jamaica's arms and stood between them like a startled hare.

"What am I doing here! I might ask you the same question, sir. I am here rightfully as the governess of these children and you are intruding on my domain. Leave this instant!"

Ignoring Jamaica completely, the man turned to the trembling child.

"I asked why you are wearing these stupid gewgaws, Caroline. Answer your father! This is not the wardrobe I supplied."

Although the words registered clearly in her mind, Jamaica's tongue seemed to have a mind of its own, reacting only to the fierceness that was devastating the child.

"No!" She placed herself between the shaken child and the man. "It is most definitely not the wardrobe you supplied. It is the wardrobe that Mrs. Greville supplied at my urgent recommendation! Salvaged from her own daughter's castoffs because you forbade that lady to purchase anything. You should be ashamed to dress your own child in widow's weeds."

He was now icily controlled. "I order you to put the young miss back into her bombazine."

"That will be quite impossible!"

"And why pray is that?"

"Because her bombazine has been burned."

His face tightened grimly. "Then it shall be replaced immediately. How dare you! I am this child's father, and I say that at five years old, she shall not be dressed in imitation of a simpering flirt."

"And I am this child's governess, and I say that at five years old, she shall not be dressed like a poorhouse widow!"

"Caroline!" He shouted formidably, and the child instantly reappeared from behind Jamaica's skirts. "Go to your room this instant and take off those ridiculous flounces and don something more appropriate."

Jamaica knelt down and caught the child in mid-flight, holding her tightly with both arms. "This child," she said, glaring up at him, "has no more idea of the word 'appropriate' than you do!"

Caroline burst into a paroxysm of helpless sobs as she clung to Jamaica. "M-m-miss Jamie, he's m-m-my father!"

For Caroline's sake, Jamaica made a supreme effort to curb her tongue. She had already said too much and assumed that she had probably lost the post for herself. But her sharpest concern now was for the child's intense distress.

The man became wooden. "You shall hear further about this," he said, ominously quiet, and hurried from the room.

Neither Jamaica nor Caroline was able to eat a mouthful of the delicious midday meal. For the rest of the day, Jamaica bent her efforts to consoling the child and deriving what comfort she could from Caroline's needful little arms around her neck. As the day progressed, she became more certain that it was her last as governess at Greville House.

Richard and Sarah questioned her with open admiration.

"What does it feel like to talk to my uncle that way?"

"Were you not terrified?"

"Uncle Charles has tantrums," Sarah giggled. "What will happen now, do you suppose?"

The afternoon seemed to drag on forever, with the two older children overexcited and impossible to control and Caroline pathetically agitated and, quite suddenly, stuttering atrociously.

By the time Caroline was asleep for the night, Jamaica was limp with exhaustion. She'd had no opportunity to speak to Mrs. Greville since the morning's incident; she had not even seen her. Returning to her sitting room, she flopped down into a chair. Assuming that Lord Dorrington would be the Grevilles' dinner guest, she did not expect to dine downstairs, and too tired to do anything else, she simply sat and waited for her dinner tray. Abjectly she looked around at the books and ornaments that she had brought with her from Biscay House and that had transformed these quarters into her home. When, she wondered, would she muster enough energy to start packing them away into her trunk. Her tenure had hardly begun and already she had ruined it for herself. She felt a deep pang of compassion for Mrs. Greville, who would no doubt bear the brunt of Greville's displeasure. And it was all her own doing. Thinking back on how the child had looked when she first laid eyes on her just three weeks ago, she wondered how she could have acted differently. Poor little darling. What would become of her now?

Her thoughts were interrupted by a knock on the door from Mrs. Pruett.

"Mr. and Mrs. Greville are expecting you for dinner, miss." The immaculate housekeeper eyed Jamaica's disheveled coiffure for a telling moment. "Maggie will bring in your hot water in a few minutes. Perhaps you'd better ask her to help you with your toilette. They've asked you to join them for sherry in the drawing room at eight-thirty. You don't have very long," she added meaningfully as she glanced at the fob-watch hanging among the keys at her belt.

Jamaica could never remember feeling less like dressing for dinner. It crossed her mind that she might decline with the excuse that she was indisposed this evening. Then, with an effort, she decided against it. If she was to be dismissed—and there was little doubt about that—it was better to get it over with. She would at least sleep better tonight. And if she was joining the Grevilles for dinner, that meant no company tonight. Lord Dorrington had, thank goodness, left the house, and she would not have to face him again. She stirred herself as Maggie brought in the wash water.

By the time she descended the staircase, just a few minutes after eight-thirty, her appearance was restored, if not her spirits. As she entered the drawing room, a hot flush rose above the neckline of her sea-green dress and up past her ears. There at the far end of the room, rising affably from his chair at her entrance, was the monstrous Lord Dorrington.

"Ah, Miss de Bowen," Mr. Greville said genially, "I don't believe you've met my brother yet. Charles Greville, earl of Dorrington."

Jamaica could not utter a sound as Mr. Greville beamed and turned toward his brother. "Charles, this is the treasure we found in Devonshire during the summer. She has already made quite an impression on Caroline, not to mention Richard and Sarah. Miss Jamaica de Bowen."

She was unable to suppress the tremor in her hand as Greville took it gallantly and brought it to his lips with a graceful bow.

"Delighted, Miss de Bowen," he murmured without a trace of sarcasm.

Feeling as if she had completely lost her bearings, Jamaica looked helplessly around the room for Mrs. Greville, but she was not to be found. There were just the three of them, and a butler standing beside the wine table. She had no idea how to gauge the tenor of the room. She missed the sense of an ax about to fall; it was as though this morning had never happened.

"I think that we might pour the sherry, John, now that Miss de Bowen is here," Greville said nonchalantly.

"Of course," his brother answered, nodding to the butler. "Elizabeth is probably making a second round of good-night kisses. She's not a great sherry lover at all events."

"You'll take a glass, Miss de Bowen?"

Jamaica could feel Greville's eyes on her bare shoulders as he addressed the inoffensive question to her.

"Yes, please," she breathed, barely making herself audible.

For more than twenty minutes, she stared into her sherry glass and concentrated all her efforts on breathing in and out, grateful that the two brothers were busily involved in a conversation about mutual acquaintances.

Presently Mr. Greville reached for his watch. "Upon my soul, I fear we shall all starve tonight if I don't go and fetch Elizabeth myself! Richard is no doubt still awake. He'll keep her talking all night if I don't put a stop to it." He downed his sherry and, to Jamaica's acute consternation, left the room.

She sat across from him, her eyes focused on the Aubusson carpet that lay between them in front of the fireplace. The long silence that followed Mr. Greville's departure seemed quite natural to Charles Greville, and the man's utter ease served only to increase her acute discomfort. Relaxed in the tall-back chair, sherry glass in hand, he stretched his legs full-length before him and crossed them at the ankle. Lazily he lifted his glass to the glow of the chandelier and admired the full-bodied amber of the wine. She was aware of his every movement from the outer limits of her vision. He twirled the sherry glass idly, and then, when she least expected it, he spoke.

"Is it a blush, Miss de Bowen, or a permanent florid condition?" His oblique gaze was quite bland, as if it were a serious question.

To cover her confusion Jamaica raised her glass to her lips, discovered that it was empty, whereupon it slipped from her fingers and fell on the carpet. Mortified, she sprang to her feet to make for the door. *Oh, he was excruciating!*

The butler watched her, expressionless.

With effort, she took a deep breath and gathering her wits and her dignity as best she could, turned to face her tormentor, who had risen from his chair with imperturbable courtesy.

"If I am to be dismissed, Lord Dorrington, I should be grateful to be informed immediately." Her voice came out less firm than she had hoped.

"If you are to be dismissed, you shall know immediately," he replied. "I am not a procrastinator."

What on earth did that mean? Surely he did not intend to overlook this morning's dreadful, heated scene? She had certainly not imagined his livid anger and his threats. Completely bewildered, she could think of nothing to say. She prayed desperately that he would make himself clear, and after a tormenting silence, he obliged.

"I have made no mention of our dispute this morning. I was possibly hasty." He frowned, and she fancied she caught a tortured expression around his mouth.

"The little moppet looked so pretty this morning," he added, as if that explained everything.

"I was unaware that that was a handicap for a female," she retorted, feeling reassured. No, she was not mistaken, in the tight set of his mouth there was a tortured look, but it faded quickly.

"I should like it to be clearly understood, sir," she continued less acidly, "that I will not countenance Caroline to be dressed in sackcloth and ashes as long as I am allowed to remain in this post."

He expelled a sharp breath and began to move restlessly about the room. "It is of no consequence to me how the child is dressed."

Jamaica barely heard the incredible statement. For the first time, she noticed his own dress. It was simple, impeccably in fashion. There was a lean elegance about him, unstudied but quite noticeable.

"Is it a habit, Lord Dorrington, or simply a hobby?"

"Is what a habit, Miss de Bowen?" he asked innocently.

"Your inclination to bully females of all ages."

"Bully?" His surprise seemed quite genuine, and she registered that his eyes were a deep expressive gray.

"Well, I simply cannot imagine any other explanation for your terrorizing an innocent child, and as for your—"

"What you can or cannot imagine, Miss de Bowen, is neither here nor there."

Then he smiled, quite disarming her, and while she stood dumbly, he took a fresh glass of sherry from the butler and handed it to her with a magnanimous gesture.

"We shall consider the matter closed."

CHAPTER FIVE

THAT NIGHT JAMAICA WAS SO RESTLESS that she left Caroline's bed after twenty minutes and returned to her own to toss and turn. If the dashing Mr. MacFarland had caused her a flurry of restless thoughts, that disturbance paled in comparison to the stormy impact of Lord Dorrington.

She reviewed the day for the tenth time. The man was preposterous! Abusive! Yet at dinner she had found him to be knowledgeable, modest, attentive—quite the perfect companion. Still, he was quite unconscionable, treating Caroline that way, treating *her* that way. It was an insupportable situation; since she had not been dismissed as she expected, she should give notice herself, in protest.

For a while she considered how it would be to return to Paignton, to wait out the dreary months until Oliver's loans were due. And then what? He would pay them of course! But what if he could not? She struggled with a wave of panic. If she gave up now, she would be a failure. No! She would not allow this beastly man to hound her from a position she handled with surprising ease and which served her very well. Besides, she realized with warm surprise, she would miss the children sorely.

Greville was not a frequent visitor at Greville House, after all; he need not affect her life here in the slightest.

As dawn crept under the curtains, she shifted her

position once more in a final effort to fall asleep. Lord Dorrington was intolerable, but she would stay with these children; she would teach Caroline to stand up for herself. Heaven knew, she would need a strong spirit, with a father like Greville.

LIFE SOON SETTLED DOWN AGAIN and the days came and went in an orderly, reassuring pattern. Two times a week, the children took riding lessons in Rotten Row. Mrs. Greville liked to watch, and took them herself. Jamaica was free for the rest of the day. She had brought her own riding habit from home, and had promised to accompany them when they had completed their first course of lessons.

As she had anticipated, Lord Dorrington was an infrequent visitor, appearing at the house once every three weeks or so when he came down to London; but except for that first time, never staying for dinner. If they met it was by chance. He never visited the schoolroom, and only occasionally made any attempt to seek out his daughter. If they met, there would be a bland good-day-to-you and a nod. That was all. He never asked after Caroline's health or progress, never sought to discuss the direction of her studies. She wanted to mention Caroline's exciting aptitude at the piano, but he never gave her an opportunity. At first his disinterest bothered her; she had expected, if not intimacy, at least something more than the cool correctness he always displayed. It was the molding of his only child that she had in her hands, after all. But as the hot memories of their schoolroom encounter faded, he became no more than a nodding acquaintance.

It was not long before Jamaica saw a link between Caroline's sporadic speech impediment and Greville's presence in the house. At times he would send for Caroline and they would meet briefly in the drawing room; on other visits they would not even see each other, but the sound of his voice, the sight of his carriage in the driveway, or just an uncanny presentiment that her father was in the house, would bring on a severe spell of stuttering that would persist until the next day. At all other times her diction was flawless.

Mr. Greville, she discovered, was a sporting gentleman, a frequenter of Gentleman Jackson's Boxing Parlor, the Westminster Dog Pits and Tattersall's. His frequent outings left Elizabeth Greville much alone. The couple rarely entertained at dinner, for the companions of John Greville's youth chose to ignore Elizabeth's existence, and the friends from Elizabeth's theater days were quite beyond the pale to Mr. Greville. There were the occasional intrepid visitors who socialized with the Grevilles, but for the most part the evening hours found Mrs. Greville alone, and she fell into the habit of inviting Jamaica to keep her company. Many an evening the two would read or sew together in the small second-floor sitting room.

By late October there were coal fires lit daily in every used room in the house. Jamaica, accustomed to the milder winters of Devon, was glad of their warmth.

"Do you skate, Jamaica?" Mrs. Greville asked one evening as they sat, chairs drawn close to the fire.

"Unfortunately not. It rarely freezes in Devon."

"What a pity. They say it will be a severe winter. I'm sure Dumbarton Pond will freeze again, if not the Serpentine itself. The children love to skate, but I fear I shall not be able to accompany them this season." She looked up from her embroidery with a quick smile "I am in the family way."

"Congratulations, Mrs. Greville! Do you hope for a boy or a girl?"

She gave a contented shrug. "Whatever comes, Jamaica. My main interest is an uneventful delivery. I'm afraid motherhood has never been easy for me. It's quite tedious, but I have to be very careful. I have miscarried twice since Sarah was born."

"I shall see to it that the children give you every consideration and do not tax your strength. When shall you tell them?"

Mrs. Greville took the tongs and added more coal to the fire. "Tomorrow, I think." She stirred the fire from its red-hot base with the poker, sending up a flurry of sparks. "Yes, I will tell them tomorrow."

"If there is any service I can perform, anything at all to make this time easier for you, please don't hesitate to tell me," Jamaica said.

"Your friendship and company is a great boon, Jamaica. I couldn't ask more from you." She stared into the flames wistfully for a moment, then returned to her sewing. "I only wish...."

"You wish, Mrs. Greville?"

"I wish my husband would accept what cannot be changed. He simply drowns his sorrows in his sporting habits, Jamaica, rather than playing out of a natural love of gaming."

"He seems to be happy enough with his winnings at Tattersall's."

"I would have done him a service if I had refused his proposal of marriage, I believe."

"But surely," Jamaica protested, "he is quite devoted to you and the children. I am sure he could not imagine life without you."

Mrs. Greville nodded. "Yes, he does love me, and he

is faithful to me. But he will never be reconciled to the fact that he is disinherited—not just himself, but his issue, too. In perpetuity. Perpetuity has such a doomsday sound, does it not?'' She smiled humorously at Jamaica, then responded to her querying look.

''When our Richard was born, it was so hard for him not to regard the child as the future earl of Dorrington. But of course it must be Charles's son, not ours, who takes the title.''

''But Charles—Lord Dorrington—has no son. The earldom is now legally his to dispense with as he chooses. If he never remarries, he is at liberty to name his nephew, is he not?''

''Neither brother would think of such a thing. Such an act would mean rescinding the terms of their father's will and testament. You must understand that both John and Charles were rather willful sons while the old earl was alive, but posthumously they have an almost morbid obedience to his wishes.''

''But if Lord Dorrington never produces a son?''

''The line will simply die out, I'm afraid. Charles will never name Caroline his heir, I know.'' She sighed. ''I devoutly hope he will marry again. His first marriage left him very bitter, of course. But I trust his sense of duty will overcome that bitterness. It's been more than five years now. It's very hard to be patient.''

Mrs. Greville was obviously sincere, her manner intense, and Jamaica wondered how it could affect her so much, since her husband's line was so permanently removed from the succession.

''Do you really care that much, Mrs. Greville?''

''Very much.'' After a long pause, she added, ''Only if Charles produces an heir will John ever surrender to the reality that he is no longer the scion of his family If

Charles never marries again, John will never give up what is a hopeless hope.''

Jamaica put her sewing aside and leaned forward. ''Surely, not entirely hopeless, Mrs. Greville. It seems to me that the late earl would have infinitely preferred your son, Richard, to succeed Lord Dorrington than no one at all. If he so treasured the title, he would not, under any circumstances, wish its demise.''

''You must realize that the blood of Norman kings runs in the Greville veins. The old man was fiercely proud of it. In Richard's veins is the blood of Norfolk gamekeepers and yeomen.''

''And the blood of those Norman kings, too!'' Jamaica pointed out. ''This is the age of reason. It is surely a preposterous idea that Richard is unfit to inherit his family's title.''

Mrs. Greville regarded Jamaica with a searching look. ''But don't you know, Jamaica, that we all live unquestioningly with the preposterous?''

For several days Jamaica's thoughts returned to that conversation. Caroline would not inherit. She would have liked to ask why, but had felt it would be overstepping the mark. Because she was female, perhaps? There was no English law that prevented it. Englishwomen frequently inherited titles, and even reigned as queens. No, it had to be Greville's personal attitude that prevented it. For what possible reason could he have such a grudge against his own child? And this blind obedience to the wishes of their late father who might possibly have been a crazed and senile old man. It made no sense.

She wondered now about her own romantic notions of love. Perhaps Mrs. Greville was right and they did all live with the preposterous. If John Greville had such deep feelings for his birthright, how consuming his pas-

sion for Elizabeth must have been, to give it up for love
of her! It was the kind of passion she had always hoped to
find, and yet, look at them! No friends to speak of, little
joy except in their children, Elizabeth alone most of the
time, her husband distracting his sorrow at the dog pits.
She sensed a deep bond of love between the Grevilles, but
where was the ecstasy? Where was the happy-ever-after
ending? The joy? It was puzzling, and not a little sadden-
ing, to witness this as a member of the household.

ON THE FIRST DAY OF NOVEMBER there were snow flur-
ries, light, fleeting, but an unmistakable promise of the
cold white winter predicted by the almanac. With the
snow came a surprise that once more lifted her spirits: a
letter from Andrew MacFarland.

> My dear Miss de Bowen,
> May I tell you how delighted I am that the centuries
> since last August have finally ground away and that
> I shall be in London in less than a week. Your Sun-
> day afternoons are surely free? I look forward with
> untold pleasure to renewing our too-brief acquain-
> tance on the second Sunday of November at four
> o'clock.
>   With salutations and bated breath,
>   Andrew MacFarland

The memory of the handsome young petty officer
came flooding back, and she discovered that she had
forgotten not one detail of their meeting. She noted that
he had left her no room for refusal, having omitted to
write a return address on the letter. She could only ask
Mrs. Greville's permission to have him call on her. He
was altogether far too forward. Could he be paying

serious court to her? She recalled the pleasure-loving gusto about the young man that belied any proper intentions. No, dalliance, she decided, was the *mot juste*.

Life at Greville House, although satisfying and very pleasant, had become a trifle tame and predictable. A little flirtatious conversation would not come amiss after all these weeks of duty, she thought. A pot of tea served in her sitting room, where she was always within earshot of a servant, was surely harmless.

"I cannot judge whether my request is proper, Mrs. Greville. Please forgive me if it is not." They faced each other over the lace tablecloth of the dining table. Jamaica had waited until Mr. Greville excused himself from the room.

Mrs. Greville regarded her with humorous dismay. "My dear, I hope you have no immediate intentions of leaving us to get married. Just when we were all getting along so well!"

"Oh, no, nothing like that! I am very happy here, and Mr. MacFarland is no more than an old family friend from Paignton," she found herself saying.

"In that case, your free time is entirely your own, to spend exactly as you wish, and this is your home now. You are most welcome to entertain your friends during your leisure, as you would in Paignton. Be sure to tell Mrs. Pruett in advance of any refreshments you would like to serve your guest."

On Sundays the children received scripture lessons from the parish vicar, the Reverend William Sump, a devout Anglican destined to remain impecunious by virtue of his modest salary and an overfertile wife. The Sumps had seven children. Faithfully each week, Elizabeth sent the young Grevilles over to the vicarage and paid two shillings a child for their religious instruction.

It was more a disguised act of charity than a sign of religious fervor. The children looked forward to it as a social occasion, which in truth it was. The vicar's children joined in the class, and there was more singing and good-natured romping than study. Traditionally, the Sump children would be invited afterward to Greville House for a huge high tea.

In the first week of November, ten-year-old Clary Sump was down with measles, and the entire vicarage was quarantined. Elizabeth Greville had developed a malaise she insisted was merely morning sickness, but by this time, Jamaica suspected it was more than that. Her eyes had an unnatural glaze, and a feverish flush suffused her face, draining away now and then, to leave her as white as parchment. On the Sunday that Mac-Farland was due to visit, she had not left her bed all morning, and the household attended the ten o'clock service at St. Michael's without her.

Driving back from church, Mr. Greville announced, "I rather fear you will have the children on your hands after all this afternoon, Miss de Bowen, although I know you are entertaining. They can't go to the vicarage, of course, and I believe Elizabeth will need to rest all day."

"It had occurred to me, sir," Jamaica said. Then, tentatively, "Perhaps the children might simply join us in my sitting room for tea?"

Mr. Greville accepted her suggestion with alacrity.

Mrs. Pruett was instructed and the children changed out of their church clothes immediately after Sunday dinner, in preparation for the unusual event.

At four o'clock they were clustered around Jamaica in her sitting room, when Mrs. Pruett brought up the visitor.

Andrew MacFarland was every whit as handsome as she remembered, as he took her hand to his lips.

"How good to see you, Mr. MacFarland. Welcome to Greville House." She grinned mischievously at his startled expression. "We have a delightful surprise for you. Lots of company this afternoon!"

"And charming company it is," he said, recovering quickly and bowing toward the goggling Sarah. He kissed her hand as he was introduced.

By the time the introductions were completed, all three children were captivated by the exciting stranger.

If MacFarland had anticipated something rather different, he was certainly displaying the utmost grace in accepting the situation, and Jamaica melted slightly as she explained the state of affairs that had led to her overcrowded sitting room.

"Do you skate, Mr. MacFarland?" Richard asked, sitting cross-legged at the visitor's feet.

"Indeed I do, sir. And you?"

"We all skate," said Sarah, patting her curls. "Even Caroline learned last winter, but—" she wrinkled her nose at Jamaica "—we probably shan't go this year. My mother's in the family way, and Miss Jamie doesn't know how."

MacFarland glanced impishly at Jamaica. "I'm sure I'd be happy to teach her."

"The pond is sure to freeze this year," Caroline ventured shyly.

MacFarland goggled at her. "You have a pond?" he said in awed tones.

Caroline nodded emphatically.

"It's so shallow it freezes very easily," Sarah explained, "but this season, mama says even the Serpentine may freeze!"

"Fancy that!" MacFarland gave Jamaica an imploring look. "Do you think Miss Jamie will let you show me your marvelous pond?"

She looked at the children. "Should you like that?" then at their clamor, "Get on your coats and hats and walking shoes. Mrs. Pruett won't be sending tea up until five o'clock. Let's go while there's still light."

As THEY WATCHED THE CHILDREN race in circles around the chilly pond, MacFarland looked at Jamaica. "I could teach you to skate, you know. Will you allow me?"

"I don't own any skates."

"No problem, Miss de Bowen. Skates shall appear like magic. Say the word, ask for the moon, and it shall be delivered at precisely this time tomorrow afternoon, wrapped in pink tissue paper."

She laughed. "I really can't say for sure that the pond will freeze, or when. Surely not until January."

"Let it freeze in January or June, I shall be here in a flash, kneeling at your feet to lace up the skates."

"Do you not have any obligations, Mr. Mac-Farland?"

"No, not to speak of. I have resigned my commission in the navy, and my only duty is to a bleak and boggy tract of Irish sod, known as Ballymere, where an ancient uncle has threatened to make me his heir. But I much prefer the pleasures of London, and I spend most of the year in my rooms off the Haymarket." He bowed low. "I am totally at your disposal."

As Caroline came running up he swept the child up with a mock growl. She screamed with delight and clasped her arms tight around his neck. Over the child's shoulder, his eyes burned fervently into Jamaica's.

"Ah, what an adorable angel you are," he said into

Caroline's ear, his eyes never leaving Jamaica's, as they all returned to the house.

Impeccably, he took his leave at six-thirty, one half hour after they had finished tea.

That evening Jamaica visited Mrs. Greville. She looked a little better than she had that morning and was sitting up sipping chamomile tea.

"I hear the afternoon was a great success—for the children, at all events. They are, without exception, thoroughly enchanted by your friend."

Jamaica was enormously pleased. "He enjoys children. I believe he is half child himself."

Mrs. Greville laughed. "Richard has announced his intention of joining the navy. Your Mr. MacFarland taught him the eight bells of the watch, and how to whistle, and—oh yes, a hornpipe. He tells me they all learned the sailor's hornpipe."

"And a sea chantey or two," Jamaica added. "I hope we were not too rowdy."

"Not at all. I am really most grateful to you for your unselfishness, and I promise that the next time you have guests, you shall have them to yourself, Jamaica."

BEFORE HIS DEPARTURE MacFarland had extracted a promise from Jamaica to go riding with him in Hyde Park the following Sunday. Now with no children looking on, it was a bold persistent MacFarland who cantered with her over the crackling leaves in Rotten Row.

It was a crisp day with a pale sun, perfect for riding, and the wide vista of winter lawns and bare trees was exhilarating.

"I shall take you to dinner at the Marquis de Sevigny Restaurant in Bond Street. We shall dine by candlelight on nectar and ambrosia," he said exuberantly, as they slowed to a trot and crossed the thoroughfare back into Kensington Gardens.

"Certainly not!" she replied.

"Surely the Grevilles can spare you! What time are your duties at an end each day?"

"When the children have their evening meal at five o'clock."

"And you are free thereafter?"

"No. I always tuck Caroline into bed and kiss her good-night at seven."

"And then?"

"Then I dine usually with the Grevilles."

"Then surely they would understand, if just once—"

"Mr. MacFarland, it is not a question of—" She stopped; she had let his insistence carry her away. "You know very well I could not dine alone with you. It would not be proper."

"Then I shall order a meal of kedgeree and eggs and bacon and coffee," he replied, smiling. "And we shall call it breakfast. You find it proper to breakfast with me, do you not?"

She reddened, remembering their first meeting, and the alacrity with which she had accepted his invitation. "Oh, sure—surely you see that breakfast at the Golden Gosling, while waiting the arrival of a hackney, is a far cry from dinner in London!"

"The Marquis de Sevigny has the best food in England. Its reputation is impeccable. Why, the Prince Regent himself favors it frequently!"

"Then I should think it would be quite clear to you that I could never be seen in such a place unchaperoned. I am the Greville's governess."

"Then you shall dine with me in my rooms. I swear no one will see us there."

"Mr. MacFarland, please be serious!"

"I am, I am!"

And she guessed that, outrageous as the proposal was, it was not altogether a jest. With MacFarland, it was so difficult to tell. He was so very rarely in earnest, always full of postures and extravagances designed to amuse.

"Ah, fairest Jamaica," he sighed, "frosty Jamaica! Would you were as warm and beckoning as your name!"

"Mr. MacFarland, if you behave with moderation, you will find me cordial enough."

"Cordial is *not* enough!" His muttered words were accompanied by a dramatically suicidal gesture, and she laughed in spite of her resolve to discourage him.

"Why have you led me on so, if it is only to plunge me into this trough of despair?"

She colored slightly. "I was not aware that I had led you on. If your intentions are less than honorable, then it is best we not meet again."

"Honorable!" he moaned. "Was there ever a man more honorable, more vulnerable, more abjectly your slave than I?"

He kept up his banter until they were outside Greville House. At the front door, he bent over and kissed her hand. " 'Til the pond freezes over, Miss de Bowen."

CHAPTER SIX

FIVE WEEKS WENT BY without a word from MacFarland.
Jamaica found herself by turns eagerly waiting to hear
from him, then chiding herself for it. She was fully
aware that he had made a most flagrant appeal to her
vanity; nevertheless, she was drawn to him.

As Christmas approached she was glad of the extra
activity that kept her fully occupied. She enjoyed the
shopping trips to Oxford Street and Bond Street and
Paternoster Row, and gave careful thought to her gifts
for the children. Finally she decided on a set of water-
colors for Richard, and a new kite for Sarah.

For Caroline the decision was easy. She went straight
to Novello's, the music publisher, and found a book of
twelve songs by Schubert for piano and voice. In recent
weeks Jamaica had discovered a peculiarity about the
child's left hand. The second and fourth fingers were as
long as the middle finger; the other hand was more nor-
mally proportioned. Caroline was self-conscious about
the oddity, although it was not very apparent to anyone
except Jamaica, who watched her finger work closely
when she played. She regarded it as a rather special gift
of nature, possibly accounting for her extraordinary
facility at the keyboard.

In the first week of December, Jamaica received a
rather doleful letter from mama about it being the last
Christmas Kitty would be at home. Since Paignton

meant a long journey and a short respite, Jamaica decided to stay in Kensington.

The holidays came and went cheerfully enough, with no sign of Lord Dorrington. Although Jamaica could not help but marvel at his total lack of family feeling, his daughter seemed perfectly content.

Mrs. Greville's health seemed to improve slightly over the four days of family festivities, but when they were over, she looked excessively tired.

With the familiar perversity of English winters, the bitter cold relaxed over Christmas; there was no snow and the pond remained unfrozen. Jamaica found herself inspecting it carefully when she walked by with the children. There was never more than a thin fragile layer of ice in the early morning that disappeared by noon. But the holly berries glowed profusely on every bush in the garden, promising colder weather still to come.

Each time she passed Dumbarton Pond, she thought of Andrew MacFarland. No doubt he had returned to his family for the holidays. Six weeks had passed without word from him—a trifle cavalier, she could not help thinking, after so pressing an overture.

Repeatedly she told herself that he was nothing but a trifler. But he was flattering and amusing to be with. She could not help but miss the gaiety his company provided, and she fell to comparing him with Lord Dorrington.

MacFarland, although he was impossibly bold, was far easier company—even Caroline found him so—than the moody Greville. If it were not for his overbearing ways and his apparent indifference toward his daughter, she fancied Greville could have been just as engaging as MacFarland. There was, to be sure, more substance to the man; he felt things deeply, she was convinced, although the nature of those feelings he kept so thoroughly hidden that one could only wonder. The petty officer, on the other hand, though slightly outrageous and always stretching propriety to its outer limits, had such flair that one could not resist going along—well, MacFarland probably never really felt at all. Or did he, too, hide his real feelings?

The children asked after him constantly, making it difficult to forget him.

On New Year's Day the temperature plummeted. They awoke to find the garden blanketed by deep snow that had fallen softly in the night. The children could hardly wait to see the pond and darted out as soon as they were dressed. Sure enough, it was at last skating-hard.

Michael, the eldest of the Sump children, surprised them all by presenting himself at Greville House before noon and offering to take the children for a spin on the ice. He had inherited a pair of skates from a parishioner's son. At fifteen, he was considered a competent escort for the children. Mrs. Greville was delighted; straight after breakfast she told Jamaica she could have the day off.

JAMAICA ROUNDED OFF a deliciously leisurely morning of reading and sewing with a brisk walk before dinner. She was returning to the house and about to cross Kensington High Street when a curricle skidded to an abrupt stop and blocked her path. The driver was Andrew Mac-Farland. Bareheaded in the open vehicle and apparently oblivious of the cold, he beamed down at her.

"Miss de Bowen, well met. I was just on my way to Greville House. I trust you are bound there, too?"

When she nodded, his hand shot out to help her into the curricle, as if they were neighbors who met daily all their lives.

She stepped up and sat beside him, too surprised to say anything.

"You see, I am as good as my word. The pond is frozen, is it not?" he said, cracking the whip over his steaming horse

She stared at him. "How did you know?"

"My dear lady," he laughed, "there is neither pond nor puddle in all London not frozen hard this morning."

"I had no idea you were in London," she said.

In reply, he reached for a package that lay at his feet and placed it on her lap. It was a box wrapped in pink tissue.

"Try these for size."

She removed her mittens and opened the package. Nestled in soft wadding and more tissue inside the box lay a pair of skates and skating boots made of fine white-calf leather.

"Mr. MacFarland, I really couldn't—" she began.

"Then I shall!" Instantly he drew rein and slipped down to his knees on the floor of the swaying carriage. "Hold this," he ordered, handing her the reins and leaving her no choice but to take them, while he unlaced the walking boots she was wearing.

Efficiently he placed one stockinged foot into the skate. She felt the cozy touch of a lambswool lining. "Oh, how lovely!" she exclaimed in delighted surprise. "It is so soft, so warm!"

"But does it fit?" he asked briskly.

Before she could answer, he pressed the emptiness at her toe. "Ah, a trifle large. The next size, I believe." He whipped off the boot and replaced her own. "I can be back in an hour with the right size skates for you. Can you take your lesson then?"

"No, certainly not," she said, for no good reason except that she was beginning to feel she was at the mercy of a cavalry charge.

"Three o'clock, then?" He stopped the curricle outside Greville House. On Jamaica's side there was a high drift of snow. She would be obliged to alight on Mac-Farland's side after he stepped down. He made no move. "Three o'clock?" he repeated.

"Five o'clock," she told him firmly.

Immediate he leaped out of the curricle and helped her down. "Good. Five o'clock." He took off again at breakneck speed, calling, "Be ready!"

When he returned at that hour, she was ready for the outing in her blue melton cape, secured at the chin, and a gay yellow scarf wound around her head. He handed her into a phaeton with boyish impatience.

As soon as they were off he grasped her hands. "Do you know how fervently I have prayed for this freeze?" The brisk manner was gone and he spoke in the hushed tones of an adoring swain. She was beginning to recognize it as a favorite pose of his and sensed a slight pricking of irritation.

"You were not obliged to wait and pray. You could have allowed an exchange of greetings between us at Christmastide. It would have been no more than civil."

"Ah, you missed me!" His voice was triumphant.

"Not particularly, Mr. MacFarland," she said, feeling her face grow rather warm.

He sighed dramatically as the phaeton drew up to the pond, then knelt to help her with the skates. As he laced the boots slowly, he said, "Strictly speaking, I am no longer MacFarland. I have recently come into my late uncle's estate. With it comes the honorific title, viscount of Kilgallen." His tone suggested that it was for some reason a very dubious honor.

"Well, now I understand your abrupt absence. Your uncle passed away. Of course! I'm sorry, Lord Kilgallen.''

He winced. "Never call me that. If you call me Lord Kilgallen just once more, I shall go straight to the Serpentine and drown myself. You must call me Andrew.''

"Andrew, then. Surely you have duties now that will allow little leisure for London pleasures.''

"Not at all," he said, grinning playfully. "I have a good steward at Ballymere who shall make my duties as painless as possible. He is the saving grace of the whole affair.'' With a breathtaking intimacy he took the scarf, which she had loosened during the ride, and caressingly rewound it around her head and neck as he spoke.

It was not until they stepped onto the ice that Jamaica realized he had devised the ultimate circumstance in which to hold her close. And she could not question it; the strange sensation of blades on slippery ice caused her feet to slide out from under her, and she was glad of his support. She was glad, too, of the woolen layers she wore beneath the melton, affording a slim buffer of propriety between her person and Andrew's arms.

Looking about her, she realized her foolishness in setting the skating lesson at five o'clock of a winter's night. The lamplighters were completing their rounds in the fading light and the temperature was dropping sharply. After a few minutes, she was dismayed to find they were alone, the stoutest of skaters having hurried back to their warm hearths. Undaunted by the raw cold, Andrew guided her firmly across the ice and around and around. After six slow circuits of the pond, she began to get the feel of it.

"I believe I can do this unsupported now," she said.

"Good for you!" He removed his arms from her waist. "I'll skate beside you."

For a few moments she glided elegantly, so thrilled with her newfound skill that she forgot the cold, then spying a dead twig, she swerved to avoid it and promptly lost her balance. He was there in a flash to catch her before she fell, and he pulled her close to him.

"You see," he whispered hotly in her ear, "you cannot, thank God, do without my arms around you."

The park was almost deserted now; she was convinced that he would kiss her as he turned her toward him. But instead, he was all business and said, "I think this is quite enough for your first lesson. We shall do this daily for a week and you will be proficient."

Back in the carriage he unlaced her skates and replaced her shoes. Then he rapped a signal to the coachman, who took off in the direction of Hyde Park.

"Andrew," she said, feeling distinctly nervous, "I must return to Greville House now."

"You shall, of course, by way of just a short turn in the park. You'll grant me that?" He touched her chin, turning it toward his face, then laid his hand on her cheek. "How cold you are!" he whispered. Suddenly his mouth was pressed to hers, and she was locked in a quite abandoned embrace.

Before she had time to struggle or protest, he released her and buried his face in the fur collar of her cape with a loud, shuddering sob.

"Forgive me. Can I help it if you drive me to distraction?"

She had the fleeting thought that they were players in a comic opera; but instead of laughing, she found herself stroking his hair soothingly, as if his dismay were genuine.

"Will you ever allow me to set eyes on you again?" he muttered in a broken tragic voice.

"Of course. You are to teach me to skate, are you not? We shall consider the matter closed." She smiled as she remembered the last time she had heard that phrase. "But in the future, we shall come here with the children."

"Whatever you say." His voice was meek as a lamb.

From that day on, Andrew became a frequenter of Kensington. Jamaica was able to enjoy his company and avail herself of his skating instruction while avoiding his more intemperate ardor, and all by the simple expedient of always having the children present. It became a routine that seemed destined to last at least as long as the winter freeze.

Andrew's company made life a good deal more interesting, particularly since Mrs. Greville was much less of a companion to Jamaica now, and in need of increasingly more bed rest.

At his request the children called him Uncle Andrew, which helped lend a thin veil of respectability to the situation. But although their constant presence kept Andrew's behavior within the bounds of decency, it did not stop his hot glances and his thinly disguised verbal advances. He was not forthcoming, however, with any honest announcement of his intentions toward her; Jamaica suspected that it was because those intentions were quite unmentionable. She did not dwell on the probability. As long as the children were present, she was quite protected.

CHAPTER SEVEN

WITH THE RESUMPTION OF SCHOOLWORK in the New Year and the diversion of ice skating, Jamaica's mind was very nearly purged of speculating on the earl of Dorrington. But in the last week of January, he paid a visit and stayed for supper.

Jamaica was invited to join the family, and once more she was obliged to revise her opinion of the man. He was genuinely cordial and came laden with belated gifts for the children. He apologized profusely for his absence over the holidays, due to a severe attack of the influenza, but was evidently well recovered that evening, and at his most lively.

There was only one occasion during the meal when she recalled the slightest breach in his conviviality.

"I do believe," Mrs. Greville said over the *crème brûlée*, "that our Miss de Bowen has been too modest about her piano teaching. Carrie is making the most marvelous progress under her tuition."

"Splendid," Greville replied rather perfunctorily.

"Carrie is the only one of us with any real musical talent. You really must hear her play sometime, Charles," she continued.

"Yes, I must," he said dully.

Jamaica had hoped that a moment would present itself when she could discuss Caroline's stutter with Greville, but already she could sense his change of mood, and she held her tongue. Perhaps a more private opportunity would occur. She had learned during the course of the meal that Greville would be staying in London for a month and that he had rented a suite of rooms in Albemarle Street.

"The children are getting a taste of the classics, too," Mrs. Greville said. "Tell him about it, Jamaica."

"I am introducing the children to the major Greek myths, and generally, to the culture of Greece. Does that meet with your approval, Lord Dorrington?"

He looked up at her, faintly amused. "I am only now beginning to appreciate the extent of your accomplishments, Miss de Bowen."

She shrugged. "Oh, I'm hardly a classical scholar, sir. It is nothing much; just some of the better-known stories, suitable for their age and comprehension. After all, they may well travel abroad when they are grown. I have sent for a book of engravings of classical sculpture that we have at home in Paignton. I think they will enjoy the pictures."

He nodded approvingly, encouraging her to continue.

"It seems that Mr. Nash has carte blanche from the prince to positively rebuild London from the ground up. I understand Piccadilly is to end in a great circle, totally after the Greek style. I think it proper that the children know that the architecture owes a great debt to the ancients. Have you seen the sketches? They were to be posted in the 'Change, I believe."

"Yes, I saw them," Greville answered. "Most ambitious." He paused for a moment as if considering something, then asked, "Have you seen the new marbles in the British Museum, Miss de Bowen?"

"Not yet, but I was hoping to—"

"They say the government paid thirty-five thousand

pounds to the earl of Elgin for them,'' John Greville exclaimed. ''And Elgin simply pirated them out of Athens.''

''He claims to have made some kind of payment to the Turkish authorities in Athens, John. Still, it is an incredible sum,'' Greville said, then addressed himself to Jamaica. ''It is said to be a quite remarkable collec tion; all that remains of the Parthenon frieze and all manner of sculpture from the acropolis.''

''Yes,'' she replied, ''there was a detailed account of the purchase in the *Western Gazette*. I saw the engravings.''

''Would you care to see the real thing tomorrow?'' he asked.

Jamaica looked inquiringly at the Grevilles, who were both nodding affably.

''I should be delighted, Lord Dorrington. May the children come, too? Richard particularly is interested in sculpture.''

''The children?'' Greville looked startled.

''Yes, I had planned to make the trip a part of their course of study. The opportunity can hardly be—''

''But the British Museum is filled with nude figures, Miss de Bowen. Hardly suitable viewing for the young.''

''Well, hardly likely to corrupt them, surely? They are masterpieces, are they not? And fashioned with the highest artistic integrity?''

''Oh, Charles,'' Mrs. Greville teased, ''let's not be stuffy about it. The children will see them sooner or later. After all, they are on public display now. I have myself seen groups of rather young children from respectable academics on tour at the museum.''

''Really?'' Greville raised his brows. ''Things have certainly changed since I was a child!''

"Charles, you have only just passed your thirtieth birthday," Mrs. Greville chided. "Do stop talking as if you were decrepit."

The look of disapproval on Greville's face was adamant, and Jamaica felt herself swept into the argument.

"The children, I am quite sure, will approach the representation of the human form with the reverence proper to God's highest creation."

Her words were greeted by one of those awkward silences that sometimes follows a burst of animated dinner conversation. She had meant to be modestly persuasive, but she was surprised how pompous the treacherous words sounded once they were uttered. Suddenly she felt absurd.

Greville managed to chew his dinner roll and at the same time lift his mouth into a look of pure amusement.

"I take it, then, you do not subscribe to the biologists who would have us descended from the apes through the blind forces of nature?"

"If you are referring to Erasmus Darwin," she said, "I have read his works and I reserve judgment. But at all events, it would not change my deep conviction that the human body is a divine concept."

"Very sensible of you, Miss de Bowen. I, who have not read Mr. Darwin, cannot speak with such authority, but I am sure the Divine Architect would approve."

She blushed, aware that she had sounded like a blue-stocking and was being teased for it. His smile was the essence of forbearance.

Still smiling he bowed toward her with the ceremonial deference usually reserved for a judge of the highest court. "It is settled then. Tomorrow's studies shall be complemented by a trip to the museum. My carriage shall wait on you at one. Can you be ready at that hour?"

"Of course. And the children?"

He gave an audible sigh. "And the children."

For the rest of the evening, Jamaica found herself repeatedly saying more than she intended and behaving in a most uncharacteristic way. She was full of high-sounding statements and bookishness. Was it an unconscious effort to set him down, she wondered. If so, it only succeeded in making her an object of his amusement. It seemed that at his most genial, he brought out the very worst of pretensions in her. It was vexing, but her tongue seemed quite beyond her control.

As she climbed into bed that night, she hoped that her performance was just a passing aberration. Tomorrow surely, the presence of the children would restore her to a more normal pattern of behavior. She had no wish to make an exhibition of herself to Lord Dorrington.

WHEN GREVILLE'S PHAETON ARRIVED promptly at one o'clock the following afternoon, Jamaica was surprised to find it empty.

"Is Lord Dorrington not to accompany us?" she asked the driver.

"Oh, no, miss. He has business in the City today," he said, closing the door after they were all seated.

"Good!" Caroline exclaimed cheerfully.

"Caroline, he is your father," Jamaica protested, "and he loves you."

"No, he isn't, and he doesn't," the child responded mutinously.

Jamaica chose to ignore the remark. She spent the brief ride discussing what they were about to see and determinedly brushing away an unreasonable sense of disappointment.

On entering the colonnaded building, they were confronted by a marble figure of Aphrodite just inside the portals. It was one-third life-size and exquisitely proportioned. The visitor's pamphlet described it as at least two thousand years old.

"Miss Jamie," Sarah declared, "she's stark-naked."

"You'll find much Greek sculpture so, Sarah. I told you this morning, the Greeks appreciated the perfect proportions of the body."

To her horror Richard snickered.

"Why is it proper for her not to wear clothes, but improper for me?" Sarah persisted.

"Because we have acquired the custom of covering our bodies for protection and for privacy. It does not mean our bodies are shameful. Don't you remember our discussion this morning?"

"Customs differ in different civilizations," Caroline repeated accurately and looked solemnly at the smooth marble. "I rather think her body resembles yours, M-Miss Jamie."

"That is indeed a compliment, Carrie, but I think not," Jamaica replied with equal solemnity. Then she noticed Richard eyeing her with the candid curiosity of early adolescence, and she hastened to redirect his attention.

"Come, children," she said briskly, "let us see what we shall find in the Elgin chamber."

By the time the carriage returned for them at four o'clock, the children were somewhat inured to nudity and thoroughly weary of looking at marble. Jamaica was a trifle let down that the children had not been more in awe of some of the priceless treasures on display. Perhaps Greville was right, after all, supposing the children to be too immature to appreciate the wonders of antiquity, she thought.

She leaned back in the carriage, thankful for the comfort of it, and watched as Great Russell Street rolled by the windows. She paid no attention to the coachman's route, and was therefore rather mystified when he halted the phaeton outside a gray stone building bearing the sign Hanberry's Coffee House.

"My lord said to bring you here," the driver announced, opening the carriage door for them and nodding toward the coffee house. "Please go in."

A plump woman in a starched white apron greeted them at the door and led them to a table where Lord Dorrington sat reading the morning *Post*.

Jamaica had felt unaccountably slighted that he had not accompanied them on their tour. Now, at the sight of him, her spirits rose, but she had no intention of letting him know it. It was an awkward moment for her, but Richard and Sarah, delighted at the prospect of tea, were boisterous enough to cover her confusion. With a smile and a bobbed curtsy to the earl, she seated herself opposite him at the round table.

A lively discussion took place between Richard and Sarah on the subject of what to order from the generous variety on the bill of fare. Caroline whispered her preference to Jamaica and otherwise remained silent.

As they waited for their coffee, hot milk and muffins, Jamaica felt obliged to make a polite reference to their outing.

"It was a most delightful and edifying afternoon, sir. A pity you could not join us."

"I believe I am beyond being edified," he answered in a bored voice, rudely continuing to read the newspaper.

Put out by his incivility, she answered quickly, "I see. You are perfect, then, and have no space for improvement as we ordinary mortals do."

He looked up quickly from the newspaper, surprised for a moment, then his eyes returned to the columns. "At any rate, I find the company of children insufferably tedious, and I daresay they care as little for mine."

"I daresay." Jamaica refrained from saying more; the serving woman was returning with a tray laden with their refreshments.

Greville's head was still infuriatingly buried in the newspaper. For a few moments she was obliged to attend to the children and their various orders as they were set down on the table. But as the serving woman withdrew and the children attacked their muffins, she could not resist adding, "Perhaps the children had better take their muffins and eat them outside? It is beginning to sleet, I see, but heaven forfend that they should cause you insufferable tedium!"

The two older children laughed noisily at this; Lord Dorrington looked up from the *Post* and bestowed a half smile.

"The tedium only becomes insufferable after an hour or so. I think this little luncheon will take less than that."

"I devoutly hope so! Eat up, children, or Uncle Charles may soon fall asleep."

Caroline took the exhortation quite literally and began to eat at an alarming speed. Sarah giggled, enjoying the buffoonery, and Richard gave his strange, high-pitched laugh.

Greville turned away from the table, ostensibly to fold the newssheet, but Jamaica guessed it was more to hide his own amusement. If he were annoyed, he would certainly not have hesitated to let her know it.

She had deliberately tried to turn his unthinking

remark into a moment of laughter. She herself was not in the least amused. Caroline had too much sensibility to bear such cruelties lightly; she had not yet recovered from her latest spell of stuttering and had so far volunteered not a word at the table. He had spoken as if he were totally unaware of her presence. How utterly heartless and stupid!

While the children turned their attention to the business of eating and drinking, she and Greville sipped their coffee in silence.

Jamaica decided she must fix an opportunity to speak to him privately about Caroline. She should broach him now, she realized. or she might lose the chance when they rose to go. His living in Albemarle Street did not necessarily make him easily accessible.

"Lord Dorrington," she spoke up at last, "could you spare me some time at Greville House before you leave London? There is something I must discuss with you privately."

"Must?"

"Yes."

His expression told her plainly that she was being very trying, but there was no turning back now.

He eyed the children, who by this time were finished eating. "Miss de Bowen, please take them to the carriage and have them wait there while you lay your 'must' before me, and get it over with."

His tone brooked no interference, no protest. It was a simple order and she obeyed in grim silence. She would have no time to think out what she would say, no time to explore the subject properly. It was not the response she had anticipated, but by the time she returned from the carriage, simmering with resentment, she knew how she would begin.

"Sir," she began, reseating herself at the table, "albeit this is neither the proper time nor place to discuss it, I must tell you that I find your disposition toward Caroline very odd, to say the least."

"You are at liberty to find my disposition however you wish, Miss de Bowen. However, it is not a subject open to discussion. Would you care for some more coffee?"

"But it is the very subject that needs to be opened. As governess at Greville House, my sole concern is the welfare of the children, one of whom is your own. I think you should know that Caroline stutters dreadfully—"

"Good heavens," he cut in, "it does not take a governess of any great discernment to uncover that! It is quite painfully clear to me that she stutters, and has always done so since she first formed words. The fact that she continues to stutter does not reflect well on you, madam. I had hoped that if you could accomplish nothing else, you could at the very least correct her unfortunate habit and teach her to speak directly."

For a moment she was confused, then, as the enormity of his misconception dawned on her, she gasped in surprise.

"Sir," she said after a moment's pause, "Caroline has no need of me to teach her how to speak directly. She speaks very well. It is in your presence, and *only* in your presence, that her tongue fails her. She has simply to learn that she need not be mortally afraid of her father, but it is not I who can teach her that."

She watched a shadow cross his face, a veiled look of pain; but after a slight pause to digest this news, his manner became very brisk. "Then, madam, there is no real problem. It is not nearly as bad as I thought. If I am the cause of her stuttering, then I will simply remove the cause. I will keep clear of her and the problem will be no more.'' He began gathering up his gloves and beckoned toward the serving woman.

''Does it signify no more than that?'' she said stonily.

''I rather thought you would wish this to be as brief as may be, since the children are waiting outside. Their welfare is your sole concern, as you have so emphatically pointed out to me.''

Throwing some coins on the table, he guided her firmly out of the establishment and into the waiting carriage. After ordering his driver to deposit the party at Greville House, he took off on foot in the other direction, leaving Jamaica too dismayed even to respond to his terse farewell.

CHAPTER EIGHT

GREVILLE'S DISPLAY OF INDIFFERENCE plunged Jamaica into a state of extreme desolation. She was hard put to explain why a man who repeatedly showed himself to be wanting in kindness, or the least trace of charity, should so crush her spirits by merely behaving with consistency; but crushed she was. Had she really expected any better of him? Had she prided herself that she could engender in him a parental concern that was so patently lacking? If so, she was a romantic fool, and that was not a consoling thought. She decided that it was her deepening attachment to Caroline that prompted her to pin her hopes on the hopeless. For Caroline's sake, she would resist all further attempts to reconcile father and daughter.

For Caroline's sake.... Now she began to appreciate Mrs. Greville a little better. Her attitude was not indifferent toward Caroline; she simply recognized futility when she saw it, while Jamaica had seen it only as a challenge to further effort.

Mrs. Greville's health was declining again, and the pervading anxiety did nothing to lighten Jamaica's spirits. In fact, such was the depth of her gloom that to divert herself, she broke a resolution. After weeks of steady refusal, she allowed Andrew to come to her sitting room for Sunday afternoon tea.

Just before his arrival, she had second thoughts and

would have sent word canceling the engagement, but she did not know his address. She waited in growing discomfort and hoped he would show no impropriety. She sought his company as a source of comfort, but it would be cold comfort indeed if he embarrassed her before the household.

When he arrived, it was as if he had read her thoughts, and his first words were designed to put her at ease.

"Never fear, Jamaica," he said, raising his hands in mock surrender, "I give you my word I shall behave."

While they sat awaiting the tea tray, his conversation was impeccably correct. Briefly he talked about his estate in Ireland.

"It is a living. The estate has a good yield—cattle, barley, thoroughbreds. Personally I prefer to see thoroughbreds at the starting gate, rather than in their laborious breeding grounds." He shrugged and his expression changed. Suddenly Jamaica could see a world of meaning distilled in the sky-blue eyes when he spoke.

"But, oh, Jamaica, if I could, I would—"

He fixed on her such an intense gaze as he spoke that she was sure he was at last about to declare himself, but the statement was left hanging in the air as the door flew open and Lord Dorrington stormed into the room.

"So!" He glared furiously at Andrew, then at Jamaica, as they sat there dumb with surprise. "This is how you spend your leisure. How dare you, madam, in this house!"

Andrew stood, a slight flush on his cheeks. "Sir, the lady is quite blameless. She was simply—"

"Abusing her position in this household. Remove yourself, sir, from this room and from this house. Now and for good."

"Now, Greville, no need for theatrics. I think we can clear this up privately without distressing the lady." Andrew made for the door as he spoke, smiling reassuringly at Jamaica. Then he stood in the doorway, inviting Greville to leave with him. "Shall we vacate the lady's rooms and discuss this elsewhere?"

"There is nothing to discuss," Greville bellowed, pushing Andrew through the door and slamming it closed.

Jamaica was gripped by such rage that she knew if she tried to speak she would immediately begin weeping. She tried to calm herself by simply staring at him, noticing that all color had drained from his face and he was experiencing some difficulty with his voice.

"This is unconscionable—that you should entertain a man alone in your rooms." He stood facing her, fists clenched, his voice barely a whisper. "As for that... that utter scoundrel, you shall never see him again. That is, if you wish to remain in this post. Is that clear?"

He waited for a reply, but Jamaica simply glared at him.

"Good day to you, madam." He turned and was gone as abruptly as he had come.

When Maggie brought in the tea tray at four o'clock, Jamaica still had not moved from her chair. She could not; her head was spinning.

"You look feverish, miss," the maid remarked. "Are you feeling all right?"

With great effort Jamaica replied, "Why, yes, Maggie, I'm quite well. I don't care for any tea, thank you. You may take the tray away."

That evening, at Mrs. Pruett's insistence, Dr. Patrick examined Jamaica and said shortly, in solemn tones,

"Influenza." She was to take to her bed and drink plenty of barley water and beef tea.

JAMAICA SUSPECTED that the cause of her malaise was frustration rather than infection, but she was decidedly out of sorts and feverish; not in the least averse to brooding for a while in her rooms as prescribed and seeing no one but Maggie, who tended her cheerfully.

She read three worthless novels and a tedious manual on wheat culture that the illiterate Maggie selected for her from the book room downstairs. She wrote desultory notes to Kitty and mama and received a letter from Aunt Kate, which alone provided some comfort.

Your stepfather has received encouraging news from the shipping office in Exeter. It seems that the *Golden Alice*, the vessel upon which ride his hopes, has left the Carolinas laden with a bumper crop of cotton. It was sighted in good trim rounding Cape Horn, and is now, God willing, making an uneventful passage through the Spanish Main and thence home via the China seas. Cautious optimism permits me to look forward, my dearest Jamaica, to your complete freedom before the end of the summer, as far as your obligation to your family and Lord Clare.

I strongly suggest that you cast an eye about you for a more tolerable matrimonial prospect, as you have no doubt discovered by now that governessing yourself into spinsterhood is not for you. You are, of course, still committed until the *Golden Alice* safely unloads at an English port, but a little speculation, since you are conveniently situated in London, will do no harm.

Lord Clare was very gratified to learn of the possibility of winning your hand in the summer. He continues in indifferent health—but he does continue.

Jamaica could not help smiling at Aunt Kate's description of the unlikely passage of the *Golden Alice*. It was so like her to get her seas confused To the urbane duchess, the world outside of English society was of no consequence whatsoever. It was evident, however, that some news of Oliver's investment had reached her, and no matter how garbled the information had become in Aunt Kate's letter, it was obviously good news.

During the rest of her convalescence, Jamaica had time to mull over her aunt's remarks. On the subject of governessing, she decided, Aunt Kate was on the whole correct. Perhaps in a different post it could be everything she had supposed, but the complexities of having two different employers, one of whom was Charles Greville, made her position one of extreme frustration. She was aware that more than once since she arrived in London, she had entertained the idea of matrimony as a possibly pleasant alternative. But to whom? Andrew MacFarland? She had always regarded him as a harmless philanderer who simply needed to be kept firmly in check. But last Sunday his conversation had taken a more serious turn. She did so wonder what he had been about to say when they were interrupted.

Now that he was banned from the house, would she ever see him again? Several times she tried to imagine not seeing him again. It would be rather like never skating again, she decided; a slight loss, but not devastating. He was not indispensable to her happiness. She realized that her chagrin sprang rather from the unmitigated gall of Greville's behavior and her own pitiful submission to it. What a poor thing he must think her, to allow herself to be used thus. She was within her rights to receive Andrew last Sunday; she had her employers' permission to do so, and she had done nothing improper. If only she had had the presence of mind to say as much at the time. But no, she had simply sat and stared at him like a china doll, and her only reaction was to become ill for a week.

By the end of the week she recovered her health, but not her equanimity. On the Saturday morning after Dr. Patrick pronounced her recovered she bathed, dressed and promptly sought out Mrs. Greville, who was also confined to her bed.

Jamaica had not seen her for many days. Although she was aware that Mrs. Greville's condition was grave, she was shocked at the change in her. Her rich dark hair was dull, and escaping from the crisply laundered bed cap, it clung in lifeless wisps over her temples. Her face was colorless and slightly puffed under the eyes, but her natural warmth was not diminished.

She brightened considerably on receiving her visitor.

"Jamaica, how lovely that you are up and about again," she said, sitting up straighter on her mound of pillows. "At least one of the invalids looks sprightly Come and visit with me awhile, my dear. It's been very dull up here."

Jamaica hesitated to burden the lady with her own woes, and she sat at the bedside, her face clouded with misgivings.

"My dear, out with it," Mrs. Greville said, interpreting her hesitancy correctly. "Something is troubling you." She smiled encouragingly. "I may be in a delicate condition, but my ears are still robust."

"May I talk to you about last Sunday?"

"Of course you may, silly girl."

"I'm sure you know that Lord Dorrington burst into my sitting room without warning, while I was entertaining Andrew, and that he created a scene."

"A scene?" It was evident from Mrs. Greville's wide-eyed dismay that she had not heard.

"He ordered Andrew to leave the house."

"My dear, I'm so sorry! He did say he wanted a brief word with you that day. It was I who sent him to your sitting room. But he was in the best of spirits—I had no idea that.... Please tell me what happened."

Jamaica shrugged. "There isn't a great deal to tell. It was over very quickly, but he forbade me to receive gentlemen in my rooms and threatened to dismiss me if I ever saw Andrew again. He called him a scoundrel."

"Oh, dear." Mrs. Greville gave a long sigh, then after a thoughtful silence, she added, "Perhaps he is falling in love with you."

"Oh, he is merely an old friend, Mrs. Greville, and I don't believe he is the marrying kind."

"I did not mean Andrew," Mrs. Greville pointed out gently.

Jamaica's brows shot up in surprise. "Lord Dorrington?"

Mrs. Greville nodded.

"In love? He does not know the meaning of the word." Jamaica looked at Mrs. Greville with renewed concern, wondering if perhaps her condition was making her delirious. But she appeared to be in full possession of her senses. "It's a preposterous thought. He hates women."

"He has not always," Mrs. Greville argued, calmly smoothing the wisps of hair back under the nightcap.

"Besides," Jamaica studied her hands thoughtfully, "he delights in nothing so much as to humiliate me."

Mrs. Greville shook her head with an amused smile. "You tend to provoke him a good deal, Jamaica."

"I? Provoke? It is only that he is so harsh to Caroline, I could not help but—"

"Can you not let it be," Mrs. Greville asked, "as I do? The child has a good home here and lacks for nothing."

"As a matter of fact, I had resolved not to press him further on the subject, but—" She stopped, wondering how to word her question, while Mrs. Greville lay back on her pillows, waiting patiently. "I have thought of you and Mr. Greville as my employers, and I have abided by the terms of my employment as you gave them. I have regarded Lord Dorrington as...as.... Does he have the power to dismiss me if I see Andrew again?"

Mrs. Greville frowned slightly. "He holds the purse strings, as you know. It would be difficult to cross him if he made up his mind that you should go." With a forefinger, she traced the intricate stitching in the quilted coverlet. "Does Andrew mean so much...?" She drew up her knees under the quilt and bounced her hands off them in a gesture of frustration. "Oh, it is too trying. You have the right to enjoy his company. He is an old family friend and I gave my consent. But since I should so hate to lose you, I suggest that you be very discreet about your visits with Andrew. For a while at least, see him only outside of this house. Do you mind?" She smiled apologetically. "Charles's storms, whatever else they may be, are always short-lived."

"Of course, I'll do as you say." Jamaica rose to go. "Forgive me for imposing on you. I will leave you to your rest now."

"I want you to feel that you can always come to me," Mrs. Greville said. "I'm glad you did."

Hand on the doorknob, Jamaica hesitated then turned back into the room. "Why did you say that perhaps he is falling in love with me?"

"Oh, nothing mysterious," Mrs. Greville laughed and spoke very lightly, as if it were of no great consequence. "One could reasonably surmise that his actions were prompted by violent jealousy."

"One could," she replied, "if one did not know that he is prone only to violent anger and not at all to love."

"Oh, Jamaica!" Mrs. Greville stretched out her arms toward Jamaica and beckoned her back to the bedside, then took her hands and gave them a warm squeeze. "I am not at liberty to divulge Charles's personal history, but he has suffered great hurt, great indignity. He may have forgotten how to show tender feelings, but I assure you he has not forgotten how to experience them. He is a good man with a deep capacity for love, a man who cherishes his family. I hope you will try to bear it in mind, no matter how trying he may be."

Their eyes met, and Jamaica saw such intensity in Mrs. Greville's expression, that she was prompted to look away as she spoke. "You have never spoken of him except with the highest regard. I respect that; it is most proper in you. And yet I must confess I cannot find him anything but odious. You say he has family feelings, but I have never known anyone less familial. And why, when he plans to stay a month in London, must he take himself off to hired rooms? A family man would find it more congenial, surely, to stay here and become acquainted with his daughter." When she turned back to Mrs. Greville, she found her face lit with an amused smile.

"You must remember that as a single man, still quite young, he has certain social needs that he could not satisfy discreetly in this house, where there are young children."

Jamaica stiffened. "You mean he has a mistress?"

"No, not a mistress. That would be too significant an attachment for him—but women, yes. Women of light virtue come and go in his rooms, I daresay. It is only natural."

"I see."

Mrs. Greville gave a heavy sigh. "No, I don't think you do, child. But trust me." She paused, then spoke quickly. "He suffered a leg wound in the war that gives him pain at times and makes him cross, in addition to—there! I have already said more than I should."

Jamaica left Mrs. Greville feeling somewhat mollified, but her opinion of Greville was unaltered. If Mrs. Greville's last words were intended to rouse her compassion for the man, they did not succeed. It would take more than an old wound, she decided as she mounted the stairs to her own room, to excuse his execrable behavior.

On the window table of her sitting room, Jamaica discovered a bowl of fresh Christmas roses. Beside it was a heavily embossed envelope addressed to her.

My dear Jamaica,
I am desolate that my presence should have caused you such distress last Sunday and, even worse, to learn that you have been quite ill. Trusting that you are recovered, I will wait for you in my carriage at four o'clock today, on the corner of Kensington High Street and Bowyer Lane, in the hope that you

may wish to take a ride through the park. Do try to come.

Andrew

HE HAD BROUGHT a soft cashmere blanket, and he tucked it around her tenderly as the driver headed into Hyde Park.

"What a blunder, Jamaica." He gazed at her with the most tender concern. "Forgive me, but it was made in complete ignorance. I hadn't the least idea that Greville was one of the—was in any way related to the Kensington Grevilles. If I had, I should never have risked your being exposed to such an ugly scene. I know the man is unspeakable."

Jamaica lowered the side glass and hungrily breathed in the sweet freshness of the park. "Do you know him well?"

"Better than I could wish. We once fought over a lady."

"You fought? You mean a duel?"

"Unfortunately, it never went as far as pistols. After the hour and the place was set, I was informed by his second that Greville had changed his mind in view of the fact that the lady was not worth a life—his or mine." He laughed. "I confess I agreed with great relief. It was the one time we ever agreed upon anything."

"But you were never friends again?" Jamaica asked, intrigued.

He gave a dry bark of a laugh. "We were never friends, ever."

His hand stole under the cashmere blanket and sought hers. "I have no intention of causing you pain by coming to Greville House again. Equally, I don't intend to deprive myself of your presence. Will you now consent to visit me?''

''Never!'' She removed her hand from his, feeling compromised even by the suggestion.

''But you will ride with me in the park?'' he persisted. ''Perhaps allow me to take you to. . .tea?''

''Perhaps.'' She experienced a wave of weariness. How long could he continue to declare his ardor without ever declaring any serious intentions, she wondered. To-day, at least, his manner was chastened. He had greeted her with more genuine affection and less coquetry than ever before, and when he returned her to Greville House, he gave her his Haymarket address with the ex-hortation that she was to send word to him if Greville caused her further annoyance.

That evening she carefully inscribed his address in her leather-bound book of friends. Whatever he had been about to say last Sunday when he was interrupted was still a mystery. He had either forgotten or thought better of it. She supposed there was still a chance that he would offer for her. She really couldn't decide whether she would accept or not, but at this point, she did not have to decide. One thing she was resolved to now: she would not let Greville thwart her chances.

CHAPTER NINE

As EVENTS TURNED OUT Jamaica need not have been concerned that Greville would stand in her way. For the rest of the winter and clear into the spring Greville absented himself from the house.

In his long absence his daughter blossomed and grew almost two inches taller. Jamaica sensed it as a season of poignant change as the child's features emerged forever from soft babyhood into a more permanent cast. Sometimes Jamaica would watch her closely as she studied or practiced at the keyboard. Still softly pretty, Caroline's face was developing a definite character. About the nose and the mouth, there was more than a hint of Charles Greville's features.

Caroline made such progress in her music that by February Jamaica could teach her no more, and recommended to the Grevilles that a music master of professional standing be hired. In March Mr. Frederick Osborne was persuaded to come weekly to the house to instruct Caroline.

Jamaica continued to see Andrew for rides in Rotten Row and walks in Kensington Gardens, mostly accompanied by the children, but sometimes alone. At every opportunity he pleaded to take her to the theater and to supper. Just as persistently she refused. Once she allowed him to take her to Vauxhall Gardens where they strolled awhile and had tea in the Chinese Pavillion, but supper, or any evening rendezvous alone with him, was a line she would not cross. His cheerful bantering was irrepressible, but she was sure he must be persuaded by now of her unassailable virtue. The fact that he still sought her company, when there was clearly no hope of a scandalous liaison, was surely an indication that he might be serious. Once or twice she wondered idly what it would be like to be the next Lady Kilgallen, but never for long. He was still a delightful diversion when she was with him, but he did not fill her thoughts when she was alone.

Richard, who had entered his tenth year and was to be ready for Winchester College in the coming autumn, was spurred to more strenuous studies in preparation for his entrance examination. Many of Jamaica's evenings were spent correcting the extra assignments she set for him in English, arithmetic and general knowledge.

On the second of April Kitty was married to Timothy Darnley. Although Jamaica's duties prevented her from attending the festivities in Taunton, she was regaled with copious accounts of the gowns worn, the food prepared and eaten, and the many fine features of Marleybrook, the country residence of the newlyweds just outside Taunton.

From Aunt Kate there was a long silence. Jamaica knew that she was busy outfitting her own girls for London, and did not expect to hear from her until they all arrived at the house on Waverly Terrace behind Grosvenor Square. The severity of the winter had put a damper on the London season. The comings out would be delayed, since so many of the turnpikes into the city were treacherous with hard-packed snow and ice. Jamaica's visits with Andrew were her only link to the social events, which, as a working governess, she could not attend.

As the winter stretched on Jamaica experienced occasional uneasiness. Playing at flirtation with Andrew and performing her daily duties could not entirely obscure the fact that this summer might just find her walking down the aisle to Arthur Sterling, marquis of Clare. It was so long ago now that she could no longer conjure up his face with any exactitude, but she could still remember her distaste. Fortunately the Grevilles did not move in the same circles as Lord Clare, so she was not often reminded of him. But although she steadfastly fixed her thoughts on a happy outcome, a promise was a promise, she would tell herself grimly. As the year inched toward spring, she was assailed by increasingly frequent moments of doubt. Even more frequently she chastised herself that she had failed to humble the haughty Greville with the aplomb she expected of herself. And now, it appeared, she had let go her last opportunity to do so.

It was on the whole a difficult year, she decided. She would not feel completely herself again until the invisible strings that bound her to an unthinkable future were cut for good.

In April a week of sparse rain gave way overnight to a hot dry spell, so sudden and so unseasonable that not a soul in London escaped the discomfort of it. Daffodils died a premature death in the bud; the new foliage in the park, retarded for so long by the hard winter, wilted and yellowed when it should have been at its greenest; apple blossoms shriveled and fell before their time; horses balked and caused an unusual number of street accidents; the children became fractious, out of sorts, and Mrs. Greville suffered acutely.

On a stifling Tuesday evening in the seventh month of her confinement, she gave birth to a stillborn girl. In an attempt to catch some breeze that airless night, every window in the house was left wide open, and Jamaica, whose room was directly above Mrs. Greville's bed, was heart-wrung by her painful cries.

IT WAS FULLY THREE WEEKS before Mrs. Greville was able to rise from her bed, but after two weeks her fever had broken for good and she had been able to sit up and receive visitors.

Jamaica brought her a freshly made sachet of lavender, the only flower in the garden to survive the drought. The pallor had not left Mrs. Greville's face, but the puffiness was gone; indeed the skin was taut and showed every bone. Her eyes looked enormous and welcoming.

"Lavender! How lovely!" she exclaimed. "I shall put it under my pillow. It's so hard to stay cool and fresh in this weather."

Jamaica sat at her bedside. "I am glad to see you recovering. What a terrible ordeal you have had."

"It is over now." She buried her nose in the lavender, inhaling the clean fragrance with great pleasure. "I have promised myself I will never be one of those women to dwell on symptoms and misfortunes." She tucked the sachet under her pillow and retied the strings of her bed jacket, smiling briskly.

"Besides, I have much pleasanter things to talk about. We are going to Switzerland for the summer," she announced, her face bright at the prospect. "Dr. Patrick prescribes mountain air for me, as soon as I am well enough to travel—and Charles insists it is to be nothing short of the Alps, for the entire summer season. Imagine!"

Jamaica responded with some polite amenities, but her thoughts were elsewhere. Greville had suggested this trip for Mrs. Greville's recuperation. He was then fully aware of the events of the past weeks. She wondered why he had not come to see Mrs. Greville in all this time.

"You and the children must escape this dreadful heat, too, of course. It looks as if Londoners will all stifle if they don't flee the city, and so...." She paused with a teasing smile that made Jamaica's heart lurch. Was she actually going to Switzerland, too? She had never in her life been farther afield than the Lake District, and she held her breath, waiting for the words. "You and the children are to leave first thing next Monday for Dorrington."

If her hopes of foreign travel had been dashed in one word, it was not disappointment that assailed her. In fact, she hardly knew what she felt, awash in a tide of anger, surprise, confusion and agitation. She found herself echoing the last word.

"Dorrington?"

"Yes, at Foxspur Park, the family seat. Charles's home," Mrs. Greville said brightly. "Quite the most beautiful spot in all Derbyshire."

She became animated as she chatted on, describing the details of the manor and the surrounding countryside in glowing terms, while Jamaica tried to digest the full import of spending an entire summer in Charles Greville's home.

After weeks of wrestling with her resentments, she had by now very nearly come to terms with him, as an unfortunate fact in absentia. The flesh-and-blood person himself she had almost obliterated for her peace of mind. And now...no, it was unthinkable. Unless Greville himself was to be elsewhere. Perhaps in Switzerland with the Grevilles, she wondered.

"Is the earl to be in residence, Mrs. Greville?"

'Oh, I should imagine so, for most of the summer.'' She paused for a moment, registering Jamaica's distressed look. "He has had his fill of foreign travel since the wars; he was quite adamant about not joining us abroad." She leaned forward eagerly, almost pleading. "You will love Derbyshire this time of the year. The house is situated on a rise in a magnificent park, and the view is. . . . What is it, Jamaica? You look so pale.''

How could Mrs. Greville be so insensible to her feelings about Greville? She groped awkwardly for words.

"It is only that. . . that he hates children. He told me so himself, in so many words.''

"Oh, the children won't bother him at all, I promise you. The house is huge, with a large staff—he scarcely need see them. I don't think he would have suggested it otherwise.''

"He suggested it?" Suddenly she found it impossible to sit still. She rose and went from the bedside to the window and stared at the streak of brightness that was the southwest finger of the Serpentine, her hands twisting nervously.

"Yes, of course he suggested it,'' the voice continued behind her, "and the summer in Lausanne. Everything is thanks to Charles's generosity. You can't imagine what a comfort he has been to John and me in our loss.''

Jamaica stood fingering the yellow-and-white calico of the summer curtains.

"Jamaica, do be a good girl now and stop fidgeting. Come back here where I can talk to you properly, and tell me what really ails you.''

Jamaica returned to the bedside feeling churlish. Mrs. Greville's face belied the brightness of her voice. The ordeal she had suffered had left its mark. One had only to look at her to know that she mourned her loss, and if she did not allow the grief to spill over to others, it was nonetheless keen for that. The lady was deriving what comfort and distraction she could from the prospect of travel; she determined not to spoil it for her.

"I apologize, Mrs. Greville. I am not quite myself. It was a slight shock; that is all. Are you sure it is quite proper for me to be staying at Dorrington?"

"Proper? Why of course it is proper! There is a married couple—housekeeper and butler—and at least twenty servants in residence. And there are bound to be other houseguests during the course of the summer. We'll send Maggie with you to take care of Caroline. You'll find it much grander than here, you know. The parklands are breathtaking, and there is a river running through the estate. But...." She studied Jamaica with deepening concern. "My dear girl, you look as if you've seen a ghost. Please rest assured I would never agree to this if Charles Greville were not a gentleman of breeding. But if you are set against it, I will not oblige you to go." The look of pleading returned. "It is all right, is it not?"

Jamaica forced a smile. "Yes, of course. It is quite all right. And I am sure you will have a delightful summer, and that the Alpine air will restore you completely."

By Sunday their trunks were packed and strapped down in the gig, ready to follow in their tracks up to Derbyshire. That afternoon Andrew took her for a ride in his splendid new landaulet, the top down to catch the breezes as they passed under the trees of Hyde Park.

When she told him, her sepulchral tone was more appropriate for pronouncing a death sentence than for a holiday. He took one look at her face, then turned his eyes to the roadway and kept them there.

"Don't look so tragic, Jamaica. No need to despair. You know I shall follow you north, do you not?"

"Oh, no, Andrew—you absolutely must not! He has forbidden you to the house; it will only make it worse."

"Dash it all, Jamaica, it was to the house in Kensington he forbade me, not Foxspur Park."

"But you know very well what he meant."

"I know only this," he said curtly, "I will not let him wreak his ugly designs on you!"

In spite of her mood she could not help but laugh at the absurdity. "Designs? He has no designs on me, I can assure you. He despises me. How could you possibly imagine...?"

He turned to her and the old, exaggerated ardor was in his eyes. "How could any man not have designs on you?" His voice had a disturbing roughness, and she was glad that he was driving the team himself, his hands fully occupied, and that half of London was taking the air in the park this afternoon.

"And you, Andrew," she said after a moment, "do you have ugly designs on me?"

He winced as if she had cracked a whip across his face. "You wound me deeply by suggesting it. Do you doubt for one minute that I am your devoted slave?"

"Yes, I very much doubt it." She let out a sharp breath, vexed by his elusiveness. "In any case, if you wish me well, you won't think of causing me distress this summer by following me north."

"Very well." For the rest of the ride he fell into a

sullen silence that made her wonder, after all, if she had not offended him.

He did not speak again until he halted the landaulet at the front steps of Greville House. "I trust you will find the Derbyshire air more salubrious than London's."

They parted thus, a chill between them, and as he drove off, she heard him crack the whip uncommonly hard over the high-stepping grays. The lightness between them that for so long had afforded her amusement and diversion seemed to have vanished all at once. The prospect of the long summer ahead did nothing to lift her spirits.

CHAPTER TEN

THEY LEFT in the cool of the morning. As they drove up through Highgate and left the city behind them, Jamaica's natural optimism seemed to seep back through her pores with the very freshening of the air. The oppressive blanket of heat that had pressed down on London for weeks appeared to lift with every mile northward.

The children were in high spirits and their laughing chatter bubbled over the sides of the open phaeton, attracting smiles and waves from every passerby, from chimney sweep to carriage folk. As they clattered their way into the deepening green of farmlands, woods and rolling downs, even Caroline was voluble, and apparently undaunted at the prospect of a summer spent with her father.

That night they stayed at a village inn outside Northampton. Supper over and the children asleep, Jamaica settled down with her copy of the London *Times*. She was stopped by the front-page article that bore a sad description of a shipwreck. A six-hundred-ton brig, the *Yorkshireman*, had foundered in a storm somewhere off the Scilly Isles. All hands were lost and nothing was salvaged but a few spars from the hull.

How precarious was the sea, she thought, and shivered. Somewhere the *Golden Alice* was facing the same unpredictable dangers that brought the *Yorkshireman* to grief. She prayed the vessel a safe journey and devoutly hoped that its master was a fine seaman.

She retired to bed early against a dawn start, but lying in the quiet country night she found herself searching her heart, indulging in thoughts she had not allowed before. Supposing ill befell the *Golden Alice*? She knew she would never fall foul of her promise. She was prepared, if it must be so, to look on this summer as her last season of freedom, and since things lay in the lap of the sea gods, so to speak, she would not let Greville spoil this precious time for her.

He was only a rather bad-humored man, she argued, not an ogre. And if she were not cowed by Aunt Kate, whom some considered the most formidable personage in society, then she could certainly stand on her own two feet with the earl. That she had tried several times and failed abysmally was true, but until now, she had never expected another opportunity to prove her mettle. The summer in Derbyshire would provide it; one last chance to persuade him that a father had certain obligations of the heart. With that thought she fell asleep.

She awoke in the predawn, calm and convinced that it was nothing less than providence that found her making this journey with Caroline. Through her ministrations she was sure now father and daughter would at last be reconciled.

It was a long second-day's journeying, with few stops, but she gave herself totally to the gay spirits of the children and arrived at the village of Dorrington jubilant, ready to vanquish all with kindness.

Mrs. Greville had not overstated the natural beauty of the countryside. Spring came late to the Midlands, and they were surrounded by a profusion of blossoming trees, narcissus and jonquils in first bloom under a sky dotted with white fluff.

Her heart lifted as they drove through the south gates of Foxspur Park and found themselves in the shade of a huge stand of newly green oaks and horse chestnuts in full bloom. As the fine gravel flew out from their wheels, the vista opened up to spacious lawns aglow with late daffodils.

Richard and Sarah began to bicker over the location of the river. Caroline, listening to each in turn, looked obediently in all directions.

"Do you remember the housekeeper, Mrs. Renfrew?" Jamaica asked the children, to change the subject.

"You mean Mrs. Posset," Richard corrected.

"No," said Sarah. "Mrs. Posset is the cook. Don't you remember the shortbread she used to make us?"

They fell to squabbling again until, after a series of winding turns, the house came into view.

"Look, children, there it is, at last."

A few hundred paces ahead lay a large gabled mansion with dormer windows and many slanting roof lines. She guessed it to be of Tudor origin, but it seemed in excellent repair and freshly painted. The horses slowed as the ascent steepened to the rise atop which stood the house. The front facade was adorned with croquet-smooth lawns broken by neat flower beds alive with spring color, and beyond them, clumps of shrubbery and a few shade trees. It seemed too welcoming, too full of lighthearted beauty to be the home of a dour widower. The approach to the portals would hearten the weariest traveler, and it reflected well on its owner; it bespoke a man of taste, of generosity and joie de vivre. Jamaica had to remind herself that this was not an accurate description of Lord Dorrington. But as she drank in the beauty all around her, she felt cheered, not only ready to beard the lion, but eager for the confrontation.

It was therefore an anticlimax to find that the master of Foxspur Park was not at home, but tending to some business in Nottinghamshire.

Mrs. Renfrew had a softer disposition than Mrs. Pruett. She made them all very comfortable, showing them every nook and cranny, and exhorting them to make themselves entirely at home while keeping up a stream of amiable conversation.

Guided by her own inclination, and by the irrepressible holiday mood of the children, Jamaica declared their first week at Foxspur Park a school holiday. After that they would begin a light summer schedule of studies, consisting of five mornings a week.

Mrs. Renfrew urged Jamaica to take the opportunity to have a complete rest herself. Jobe, the head groom's son, would take the children riding whenever they wished, and between Maggie, Mrs. Posset and Mrs. Renfrew's crew of servitors, every minute of the children's day would be accounted for.

Jamaica readily relinquished her responsibilities for the space of one week, and Mrs. Renfrew was as good as her word. The children were occupied, entertained, supervised and coddled. Relieved of all accountability, Jamaica found herself enjoying a pleasant, if rather solitary, holiday. A gig and a riding horse from the stables were put at her disposal. She rode the woodlands and lanes surrounding Foxspur, and covered miles on foot within the boundaries of the park. The river, buried in a dip behind the house, flowed gently between winding willowed banks and offered secluded bowers of dappled shade where she could sit and read undisturbed for hours at a time.

Her evenings were spent in the congenial company of Mrs. Renfrew; Jamaica welcomed the company and the informative conversation. Greville, she learned, had inherited a Nottingham coal mine as part of his father's estate. The pits were old, gutted for several layers, and more trouble than they were worth. The earl had kept them open for the sake of the miners, who had little chance of employment elsewhere. It was taking more and more of his time and money to shore up the crumbling pit walls and prevent accidents. It was what was currently keeping him from Foxspur; he was expected home the following week.

The housekeeper was inclined to refer to her master as "a dear good man who deserves a happier lot than this."

"We're all hoping he'll find a gracious lady who'll make him happy again," she told Jamaica, "but it won't be easy to find one good enough!"

Knowing a very different side of the dear good man, Jamaica kept her counsel and let the words flow by. She drank in the verdant beauty of Foxspur, wrote leisurely letters to Kitty and mama describing it all, and read to her heart's delight from a well-stocked book room. Each morning she was awakened at nine with a breakfast tray prepared by Mrs. Posset.

By Saturday she was so indolent that when Mrs. Renfrew suggested taking the children to church with her on Sunday morning so Jamaica could enjoy her last lazy morning, she readily agreed.

It was ten o'clock before she was up on Sunday. She took a book and went down to the river to spend what was left of the morning under her favorite willow tree.

She had chosen the book carelessly. It was a worthless romance, insipid from the first page. It was not typical of the book room fare here, and she turned curiously to the flyleaf. An inscription read: Stella Greville, Countess of Dorrington. Was she his late wife or his mother, she wondered.

Disinclined to leave this spot and return the book to the house, she laid it aside, stretched out on the soft grasses, and watched the clouds drift by. Stella. . . if it was his late wife the lady was very fluffy in her reading taste, not quite the spouse she would have imagined; but then it was hard to imagine Greville espoused at all. *A man who cherishes his family,* Mrs. Greville insisted. Could it be the loss of Stella that had so disfigured his heart? Lazily she began to daydream, spinning romantic fantasies around Greville's mysterious past. She was deep in idle reverie when she heard a voice directly above her.

"I am glad to see you earning your keep!"

She sat bolt upright and found herself in the looming shadow of Lord Dorrington. Embarrassed, she got to her feet, brushing away the grass from her calico skirts.

"Good morning, sir. Please excuse my appearance. I declared a holiday for the children this week. It seemed appropriate for their first week in the country."

He stared at her neutrally while she babbled.

"Mrs. Renfrew said I should take my ease for the week," she added defensively.

He looked exhausted; there were lines running from his nostrils to his jawline, and his cheeks were gaunt. She readied herself for a sharp retort, but he said only, "Then take it. Take your ease. I will see you at supper." Then he turned on his heels, following the river bank in long slow strides until he disappeared behind a clump of willows.

She was left feeling vaguely uneasy, her head full of questions. How long had he been home? Last night? This morning? Was he inviting her to sup with him this evening, or did he simply plan to call her to account at that time? And for what? For behaving like a house-guest instead of an employee? Could he disapprove of the children taking an early summer holiday? Surely not, and if not, what was she supposed to do?

At dinner some of her questions were answered by Mrs. Renfrew. The master had returned late the night before and had let himself in without announcing himself, the household being asleep. He had said there would be two for supper, and so yes, she was invited to join him at table.

She spent an industrious afternoon in the second-floor sitting room that was to house their school activities through the coming weeks. The school supplies were still in a trunk, and she worked at unpacking and arranging them so that they could begin their lessons smoothly the following day.

Jamaica had the better pieces of furniture removed, along with the carpets, and Mrs. Renfrew found her some waterproof sheets to spread under the three card tables that were to serve as the children's desks, thus protecting the floors from ink spills and crayons.

There was a fragile Hepplewhite escritoire that would serve as Jamaica's desk. The window had a good north light, and she arranged the furniture so that they would all be well supplied with daylight.

There was much she had neglected, and she worked steadily until seven o'clock, when Mrs. Renfrew appeared.

"Have you finished, Miss Jamaica?" she asked. "I've had a bath drawn for you."

Jamaica nodded gratefully. She was to join Greville at eight o'clock for supper. Hastily she put the finishing touches to the schoolroom and left to bathe.

As she soaped herself in the zinc bathtub, she mulled over her findings. In the little sitting room she had used a carved mahogany chest for storing some volumes. The chest had been empty save for one book, another insipid novel very like the one she had begun to read that morning. Its only interest to her was the flyleaf inscription: *To Stella from her adoring Charles, November 1805.* From the date, she knew now that Stella was his late wife.

As she dressed for the evening, Jamaica tried to reconcile the man who could describe himself as "adoring Charles" with the man she knew as Charles Greville. It was an impossible task for the imagination. But by the time she had dressed her hair and fastened the last button on her rose muslin, she felt more kindly toward him than she had done for some time.

Supper was served in a small room off the library. There was no dumbwaiter down to the kitchen; the meal was to be quite informal, Mrs. Renfrew explained. Lord Dorrington preferred to sup there when there were no guests, and to serve himself from a dinner cart.

There was a wood fire burning in the grate, crackling with pine needles. A small table, set for two, was drawn close enough to the hearth so that the silver candlesticks glowed in the firelight. Someone had neglected to draw the curtains. She entered the room to find the earl staring out of the blind windows that gave onto a paved terrace, but now after darkfall, reflected only his image and the glint of his brandy glass.

He ignored her, or perhaps did not hear her enter until she spoke. "Good evening, Lord Dorrington."

He turned quickly, his brows slightly raised, as if he had not been expecting her, and then suddenly remembered. "Evening," he muttered, then stirred himself to some semblance of hospitality. "I'm drinking brandy. Will you join me?"

She had the fleeting thought, *Men who drink brandy before supper*...then suppressed it. "Some sherry, if you please." She tried to sound neutral, but his eyes seemed to penetrate her thoughts.

"You disapprove?"

"Of brandy? Hardly, my lord. If you feel the need of it, it is not for me to approve or disapprove."

"Ah, if I feel the need of it," he mimicked. "That is exactly what I feel, Miss Propriety."

Jamaica flushed as the footman handed her a sherry glass.

"Tell Mrs. Posset to hold supper until I ring," he told the footman. "Then you can retire, Jim. We'll serve ourselves."

As the door closed behind the servant, he gulped his brandy down and stared at her accusingly across the room.

"Have you ever seen a case of black lung, Miss de Bowen? No? What a sheltered life you have led. Black lung is a coal miner's disease. No, you would not have seen it, coming from the sea-swept West Country. They get it when they're thirty or so. They slowly choke to death."

Jamaica shuddered inwardly. There was no hint of compassion in his voice as he swirled the remaining liquid in his glass. He spoke with a strange brightness, as if this were a typical social supper conversation. It was bizarre. Horrid.

"You've never heard the cries of an eight-year-old

caught in a collapsed seam with his bones crushed? Heavens, yes! I feel the need of brandy." He drained the glass and went to the wine table where the brandy decanter stood among the light supper wines.

As she watched him refill his glass a little unsteadily, she said, "Mrs. Renfrew told me you were consulting with the engineers. I had no idea you witnessed a disaster. I'm so sorry."

He gave a snort. "Don't be. Don't waste your pity on me, madam. As you can see, I am in good health."

"No, I meant...." She groped for more appropriate words, something to ease the tension in the air, but he dismissed her effort with a jaunty wave of the hand.

"A disaster is a commonplace in Burchdale. But I'm closing the pits down; should have done it two years ago, but for—" He stopped, pressed his fingers to his temples and shook his head, as if he were shaking off a nightmare. "I apologize. This is no topic for a lady." He emptied his second glass of brandy, set it down and took the decanter up once more. "We'll talk of other matters," he said amiably.

"Oh, please," she protested, "if it eases you to talk of it, do not—"

"We will talk of other matters." He lifted the decanter as he spoke and slammed it down on the table so hard that it cracked.

"You will oblige me by pulling the bell," he said, pointing toward the cord that hung by the hearth where she sat. As he gestured he brushed some of the tall stem glasses with his sleeve and they fell with a sound of shattering crystal, one rolling off the wine table onto the floor.

"We had better eat."

Jamaica pulled the cord, panicked at the thought of

staying here to eat supper with a man obviously in his cups and becoming more morose by the minute.

When the food arrived and the broken glass was quietly cleaned up by the self-effacing Jim, they seated themselves at the table, and he seemed to mellow.

There was a cold consommé and a curry of veal kept warm in a chafing dish. They spoke only about the food for a while, as if it were of intense interest to both of them. When that topic was exhausted, they lapsed into a silence that Jamaica found intensely disturbing. Presently she decided to break it.

"I hope it did not bother you that I took my holiday here while the children took theirs," she began.

He shrugged and remained silent.

"Mrs. Greville offered me leave to return to my home, but I decided not—" She stopped abruptly, remembering why she had decided against a holiday: she had not wanted to leave Caroline at the mercy of her father.

He was staring into his plate, pushing the veal around the dish with his fork. "Why should your holiday bother me? Nothing bothers me."

The air in the room seemed to crackle. She felt she was seated in front of a powder keg with the fuse lit and burning erratically. She willed him to eat something and sober up. She gave her attention to her own plate and swallowed some food with a conscious effort of throat muscles.

She watched him, endlessly rearranging his food on the plate, until suddenly he stopped and threw the fork down on the white tablecloth, spattering it with a bright saffron stain.

"You think I'm a cold fish, do you not?" His expression was grave, his eyes the color of the sea at dusk, sternly demanding an answer. He seemed suddenly very sober.

She felt impelled to answer him with absolute honesty.

"No, Lord Dorrington," she heard herself saying, "I do not think you are a cold fish. On the contrary, I am convinced that you feel things very deeply."

"Then you are absolutely wrong! Whatever feelings I may once have possessed as a foolish young man are now numbed forever in a bottomless glacier, and I am therefore your complete cold fish."

"I doubt it," she told him, "but even if it were true, it does not excuse your coldness to your daughter. I, at least, find that inexcusable."

"Ah, yes!" At last he took a morsel of food and chewed it, nodding thoughtfully. "That would be inexcusable," he swallowed, and fell to forking his food idly around the plate once more, "if she were my daughter."

What rubbish was this, she wondered, elaborately applying her serviette to her lips to play for time. Did he believe he could knock a kinship out of existence by a deliberate lack of sensibility? Did he think a kind of emotional surgery obtained because he wished it so, like a field surgeon lopping off an offending limb? Now it is there, now it is gone? She decided she would not allow herself to be fenced with.

"Sir, one cannot destroy a fact of birth. It is so and it will always remain so."

"Precisely."

The razor-sharp edge to his voice made her look up quickly. He had not been speaking figuratively. That he was no father to the child in the dutiful sense was not news to her, but this was; was he saying that he had not even sired her? That was unthinkable. She had seen the lineaments in Caroline's face so clearly. Or had she merely imagined them? She was so shocked that before she could consider what to say, she found herself blurting out a dismayed question.

"But if she is not your daughter, then whose?"

He clenched his fists and rose from the table so fast that he tipped over his chair. Impatiently he kicked it out of his path and strode toward the French windows, his face turned away.

She watched his back anxiously as he stared at the leaded panes. He breathed heavily, trying to master his rage, his sorrow, whatever it was that made his shoulders heave. After a few moments he seemed to calm himself and his shoulders relaxed. He opened the windows wide and allowed the chill evening to sweep silently through the room as he returned to the table and righted his chair.

He sat down and immediately reached for the wine decanter. As he refilled their glasses, his hand shook slightly, but his voice was firm.

"As to your question, madam, it is unanswerable."

Jamaica felt stifled in spite of the open window. "Please, it was gauche of me. I had no right to ask."

"Not at all," he said, unruffled and entirely reasonable. He stopped to drink off the tall glass of wine as if he were quenching an insatiable thirst. "You have the right to know exactly who your charge is. As I have the right to know exactly who my daughter is. Only I don't—she isn't." He closed his eyes and opened them as if to clear up his own confusion. "You see, Miss de Bowen, my wife had very catholic taste. Caroline's father might be one of several gallants who enjoyed her favors. She was most generous."

Jamaica struggled with her feelings; she felt a strong

wave of compassion for this tortured man. But Caroline was an innocent child, no matter who her father was. It did not pardon his cruelty. She must make him see.

He mistook her silence for shock, and his mouth lifted ironically at the corners.

"Do you not grasp my meaning, Miss Propriety? I am informing you that my late wife was an adulteress. But I suppose it does not signify. Most women are at heart."

"I think you have no proof that Caroline is not yours. If you were with her often and knew her as I do, you would surely see—"

He shook his head to stop her. "Legally, of course, she is mine. She bears my name and I provide for her generously. But as for the blood kinship—" he shrugged carelessly "—the odds are against it."

"How utterly..." she began, then petered out, unable to find words adequate to express her feelings.

"How utterly what? Utterly scandalous? Utterly immoral? Utterly beyond the pale?"

She shook her head. "I was going to say, how utterly sad. That is all."

"Sad?" His manner was quite easy now, as if he had breached a wall of reserve and meant to keep it down. "By no means sad. Caroline is hardly a waif in the streets. She will never lack for a roof over her head or a fine carriage to ride in. Sad!" He gave a dry laugh. "You talk as if she wanted for nourishment."

"There is another kind of nourishment, sir. Every child has a right to it. The nourishment of the heart."

"Well, we must each find that where we can."

He tried to stare her down, daring her to pursue it further, but she met his gaze evenly, determined not to let it go at that.

At length he threw up his hands in exasperation. "For God's sake, what do you want of me? Her paternity is questionable, she had the poor taste to be born a female, and to put it short, I cannot stand the sight of her. What would you have, madam? Would you have me dote upon her?"

Jamaica sat silent a moment, acknowledging defeat. There was no hope at all. She was at once very tired. "If you would excuse me, sir, I should like to retire."

"No!" he shouted, "I shall not excuse you. You shall show the civility of staying here and finishing this meal with me. Ring the bell. It is time for coffee."

She rose to do his bidding and could not escape the feeling that his eyes were upon her as she went to the hearth, watching her move.

When she rejoined him at the table, he eyed her coolly, very self-possessed. "Of course, I shall remarry," he said matter-of-factly. "There is no other course open to me if my line is to be perpetuated."

Jamaica cringed at the thought of Greville with children he would acknowledge as his, while Caroline continued as far away as possible, kept from his sight like something disreputable

"And who is the fortunate lady?" she said bitingly.

He thumped the table and laughed. "You have a knack of asking the unanswerable tonight. I haven't the least idea who the fortunate lady shall be. Nor do I care the slightest, so she be a good breeder of sons, and not so desirable that her constancy may be put in question." He spoke defiantly, staring with knitted brows as a servant entered with the coffee tray, laid it on the sideboard and began to clear the dishes from the table.

Jamaica felt her stomach turn in disgust and was glad to have a pretext for leaving the table. She went to the sideboard, fussing with coffee spoons, pouring out two cups and bringing them to the table.

They stared at each other in silence until the servant left. The table had been cleared of all but a pile of dessert grapes. She stared at her coffee cup in dismay. She had unthinkingly added cream when she preferred it black, and she became aware now that she had been distractedly adding spoon after spoon of sugar to it, out of nervousness. She took a sip and shuddered at the awful sweetness.

"And how do you propose to find your ideal bride?" she burst out angrily. "Will you advertise in the newspaper for a plain, fertile woman, then line up all the respondents in the cow shed and make your choice?"

He failed to suppress a slight smile. It was as though he had expected to silence her once and for all with his outrageous words, but could not hide his admiration for such a gallant sparring partner.

"I have left the matter entirely in the hands of a good friend; a friend of my late mother's. I believe I can trust her judgment."

"Then I wish you good fortune," she said tartly, and drank off the rest of the coffee before she remembered how it tasted. She spluttered, started to choke and left her chair. She made for the wine table where there was drinking water in a pitcher, and as she did so, she stepped on a shard of broken wineglass embedded in the carpet. It pierced the silk sole of her slipper and entered her foot. She cried out in pain, and leaning on the table, bent to pull the offending sliver from her foot.

Greville was immediately by her side. He helped her hop back to her chair.

"Let me see," he said, removing her slipper and squatting down with a clean napkin in his hand.

The glass had torn a hole in her silk stocking. There was a small trickle of blood. He squeezed the wound. 'I don't believe there's any glass left in your foot. I'll bind it with this, then when you get to your room, you should bathe it.'' As he spoke, he tied up her foot in the napkin.

"Can you stand?'' he said as he straightened up, holding out his hand.

"Yes, of course. It's nothing,'' she said, ignoring his hand, relieved to have an excuse to leave the room at last.

But when she tried to stand, she could not do so without his help.

"You had better not walk on it until it feels right,'' he said, lifting her off her feet and carrying her toward the door. His manner was brisk, kind and a little embarrassed, as if he were awkward at being caught displaying any human concern whatsoever. She was so intrigued by the sudden change of manner that she simply watched what was happening in a detached way.

At the door he waited. Vaguely she wondered why, until he said quite mildly, "Would you mind opening it?''

It was quite obvious that if she extended her right arm downward, the door handle was within her reach. It was her turn to be embarrassed. Turning pink, she opened the door and allowed him to continue his progress down the hallway to the staircase.

He took the stairs easily, but paused at the first landing. "You would make my task easier if you would hold on,'' he said.

She hesitated, until he added impatiently, "Put your arms about my neck, you silly goose. I'm not about to rape you.''

She obeyed, supporting some of her own weight, and ne continued more easily up the second flight and the third.

"Which room did Mrs. Renfrew give you?"

She pointed down the east wing and he followed until they came to her door. This time she remembered to open it. He entered and deposited her carefully on the edge of her bed.

"Do you need further help?"

"No, I'll be fine, thank you."

"Well, if you find yourself in further need of assistance, do not hesitate to ring for a chambermaid. If you need a physician, Mrs. Renfrew will send for one. Good night."

His manner was so impersonal that she felt close to insulted. As he stood by the open door, he turned toward her once more.

"Please accept my apology for anything I may have said this evening that you found untoward." He paused, and when he spoke again his voice was very low. "Yesterday I attended the burial of five miners. One of them was but eight years old. I have been drinking more than is customary for me "

A deep wave of feeling washed over her, a need to comfort him. But he was gone before she could respond.

The scratch on her foot was superficial, but her stomach was very queasy. All night she twisted and turned, her feelings swinging with the regularity of a pendulum, between disgust and pity for the strange master of the house.

CHAPTER ELEVEN

THE NEXT DAY she learned that Lord Dorrington had left again for another business trip to Nottingham, and so the week passed pleasantly enough: mornings in the schoolroom, afternoons at her desk preparing the next day's lessons and marking papers, when she was not supervising Caroline's piano practice. The child was a conscientious student, and it had become pleasurable to listen to her play.

There were one or two callers during the week, who were informed that the master was away. Jamaica discovered that all the comings and goings at the front door of the house were plainly audible from the schoolroom. With the front windows open, one could hear the carriages draw up, and the conversations under the porte cochere. It was one of the few drawbacks of the room; she was obliged to discipline the children's curiosity and return their attention to their work.

On Friday morning the maid who woke her brought the news that Greville had returned. She did not see him, and as she began the morning's lessons, she was distracted by the thought that he might invite her to sup with him again. She did not relish an ordeal such as she endured the previous Sunday, yet she knew that if he did not approach her, personally announce his presence or invite her to eat with him, she would be vaguely disappointed.

Nonsense, she told herself firmly, and turned once more to the blackboard and the rivers of England, which the children were committing to memory.

Sometime during the morning, she heard the crunch of footsteps on the gravel—a gardener perhaps, or Greville out walking. She suppressed a childish desire to stand up and look down from the window. She had been so insistent all week that the children not jump up and peek at the source of every sound below.

She heard voices and strained her ears to catch fragments of a rather quiet conversation...settlements, liens, contracts of sale. Greville, she guessed, discussing his affairs with a steward or a solicitor.

It was not until almost dinnertime, when she was ready to clean off the blackboard and dismiss the children from class, that she finally allowed herself to steal a look below. Greville it was, seated at the terrace table with a large pile of papers. He worked quietly in the morning sun; whoever his companion had been, he was gone.

Turning back to the children, she brushed the chalk from her hands and said, "You have no homework today. Perhaps Jobe will take you for a boat ride after dinner. Go and get ready."

She wondered whether Greville heard murmurs of their conversation as she had heard his. The room was very quiet after the children left, and she fancied she could hear hooves coming along the south driveway. She looked out once more, but there was no sign of anyone, just Greville, quietly studying his documents.

As she began to tidy up the room to leave it ready for Monday morning, the sounds of a horseman grew louder. She had not imagined it. A single horseman was cantering up to the house at considerable speed. She would not be a curious face at the window, she told herself, and continued about her chores, gathering up the children's school smocks to take down to the laundress.

"MacFarland, what the devil are you doing here?"

Jamaica dropped the armful of smocks in surprise, then froze.

"The name's Kilgallen now, Greville."

There was no mistaking the voice. It was bold, cheerful and, she suddenly realized, infinitely welcome.

"Your name may change with an inheritance, but the fact that you are both uninvited and unwelcome here does not change."

"Oh, come, Greville, I thought you'd come to your senses by now."

"I never left them."

"My dear fellow," Andrew sounded placating, "all I want is to pay a short call on Miss de Bowen. Let her know I'm in the neighborhood for a few days. You can't possibly object to that!"

"Miss de Bowen is not here."

Jamaica was shocked at the ease with which he spoke the lie.

"She has left my brother's employ and has taken herself off, I know not where," the cool voice continued. "And you would oblige me by doing the same."

"I don't believe you, Greville." Andrew's voice rose in anger. "She told me herself not two weeks ago that she would be spending the entire—"

"You may believe what you like," Greville cut in, "but if you don't leave this instant, I shall have you forcibly ejected. And the next time you invade my property, you shall be greeted by the hot end of a musket."

There was a brief silence, then the sound of loose gravel, the single crack of a whip, and then hoofbeats retreating down the carriageway at an angry gallop.

Jamaica left the room and broke into a run along the passage, down the main stairs to the front door. She would show herself to Andrew and prove Greville a liar. She rushed through the front door and across the terrace, but horse and rider were already out of sight. Ignoring Greville, she began to descend the terrace steps, calling his name.

Greville caught her roughly by the arm. "No!"

She turned furiously and wrenched her arm from his grip. "How dare you lie about my presence here! How dare you meddle in my affairs!"

He blocked her path with his body. "I dare because I am responsible for your welfare, just as you are responsible for the children's."

"I am no child! The conditions of my employment have never precluded my having friends of my own choosing. I am a grown woman."

He gripped her arms roughly and shook her in exasperation. "Then behave like one! Andrew MacFarland is no one's friend. Don't you know that he is a scoundrel? Infamous for his seductions? That is all he wants of you or of any woman."

"Let go of me," she shouted. "I know how to handle my affairs. Do you take me for a light-skirt?" She struggled fiercely, but he had gripped both her arms in an iron vise

"Do you actually suppose yourself to be above the persuasions of the most accomplished seducer in London? Are you inviolable?"

"Yes! And if you do not—"

"*Idiot.*"

She got no further in her argument. Greville stopped all further words by pulling her to him in one swift movement and closing her mouth with his. He held her thus, struggling vainly to free herself for what seemed like minutes, until she became aware that she was no longer fighting him, and he was no longer using force to bind her to him. What had begun as an angry assault to block her flight had turned into the most tender of kisses. She was bemused to find her arms locked tightly around his neck, but she was too swept up to question it.

She had the strange but distinct sensation that she was home, where she had always belonged. He was no longer hurting her arms with his ironlike grip, but was clasping her to him with a delicious, fierce tenderness she had no desire to stop. His clean-shaven lips brushed hers sensuously, leaving them for moments, only for the joy of renewed contact. Her body glowed with the ardor of it, pressing forward openly for more.

When he released her unexpectedly, she had rendered herself so yielding that she toppled forward, resting on his breast. Gently he propelled her away from him and steadied her on her feet.

She opened her eyes eagerly seeking his for what she knew would be a reflection of her overwhelming discovery. But his eyes were opaque, unreadable, a hard crystal under smooth, carefully composed brows.

"*He* is far better at this sort of thing than I, Miss de Bowen." He spoke slowly, his voice very soft. "A true virtuoso. Do you still believe you are impervious to the risk of seduction? If so, then you have nothing to be concerned about. Go after your 'friend' without compunction." He turned away from her. "As you say, you are a grown woman."

Jamaica recoiled as if stung by a serpent and watched incredulously as Greville seated himself calmly at the table on the terrace and resumed the study of his papers. He seemed no more disconcerted than if he had simply interrupted his work to swat a fly.

Her pride stirred painfully, and before he could notice the welling tears, she blinked them back and fled blindly into the house, brushing past a servant and almost knocking him down in her haste.

When she reached the privacy of her bedroom, she allowed her mind to evaluate the tumultuous experience. She had actually been gulled by his fiendish tactics. She had let herself believe that Greville's gesture was a genuine one, that his actions toward Andrew were prompted by jealousy and that his feelings were hotly engaged toward her. She had been monstrously, unspeakably tricked. It was nothing more than a cold demonstration of her vulnerability toward him, toward Andrew, toward any likely man who laid his vile hands on her. She was just a poor, stupid creature who could be seduced by the most patently contrived advances. That was the sum of Greville's message.

It was well taken. A sob escaped her, and then as the full extent of her mortification swept over her, she began to weep bitterly, controlling herself only long enough to inform Mrs. Renfrew, through the closed door, that she would not be down to dinner because she was not well.

When she had done crying over her humiliation, she thought of the marquis of Clare and wept again over the horror of such a marriage. Then she wept over Mrs. Greville's lost child, wept for Caroline. Her immediate world became a sea of tears, held back for so long that it seemed now the dam was open nothing would stop them. When at last she had cried herself empty, Mrs. Renfrew came in and brought her a cool towel soaked in cologne. Jamaica applied it to her hot face.

"My poor child," she said, drawing up a chair beside Jamaica, "was it very bad news you just received?"

What should she say? *Lord Dorrington kissed me and I am desolate? Your master is a fiend who has harassed me since I first laid eyes on him? With the help of your dear good master, I have made a complete fool of myself?* No.

Still hiding behind the towel, she said in a muffled voice, "Thank you for your concern, Mrs. Renfrew. It is nothing. I will rest awhile and it will pass."

"Very well, dear." Jamaica heard a slight scrape of the chair as Mrs. Renfrew rose. "Then I'll see you're not disturbed."

Having cried herself dry, Jamaica bathed her face in cold water until it was more or less restored to its usual color and shape. Then she went to her portfolio and drew out from a bundle of envelopes, the last letter from Aunt Kate. It was dated April 29, almost two months ago.

My dear Jamaica,
The girls and I are at last safely arrived in Waverly Terrace, and about to launch into another of the London seasons you despise so.... Your mama and step-papa are in good health and spirits. No further news on the *Golden Alice*, which in itself is, I suppose good news...

It was a long and amusing letter with gossip about the family and Kate's daughters, and ended with a veiled exhortation:

I am most anxious to hear if you have done as I suggested and cast a speculative eye around you, although I am painfully aware of the limited opportunities that exist in the social position that you have chosen for yourself.

Coming as it did on the heels of the baby's funeral and Mrs. Greville's illness, Jamaica had never answered the letter. Only now did she notice the quality of the paper; it was not the good linen stationery that Aunt Kate always used, but a plain, rather thin sheet, already cracking at the folds after two months. The letterhead did not bear the heavily embossed crest of the de Bowens. It looked more suitable for a casual note to a tradesman. Was Aunt Kate trying to impress on her the humbleness of her present position?

Feeling extremely dejected, she got out paper and ink and sat down to write to Waverly Terrace.

My dear aunt,

As you will see, I have been sent with the children to Derbyshire to spend the summer in the house of Caroline's father. I find myself now in the situation of being solely accountable to him and it is an intolerable one. The earl of Dorrington is a quite impossible man. I believe you were right in your judgment, dearest aunt. Governessing is not for me, although I love the children dearly and was tolerably happy at Greville House. I find myself absolutely obliged to give my notice.

Please expect me at Waverly Terrace within a few days of receiving this. When it is posted, I shall straightaway begin to pack and make immediate ar-

rangements to book the first available passage on a
hackney to London.

As for the future, please be assured of two
things. First, I shall not impose on you long at
Waverly Terrace, but will simply break my journey
there and thence return to Paignton; and second, I
am aware that the outcome of Mr. Canwood's investment should be clear very soon. Either the
vessel will arrive before the notes are due, or Mr.
Canwood will be obliged to honor his debts in a less
desirable way, and I shall be obliged to honor mine.
I have no thought of reneging on my promise to
you. To be the wife of Lord Clare could be no
worse than the humiliation I have suffered in this
household.

Meanwhile, my fondest wishes to the girls and to
you, until very soon.

Your affectionate niece,
Jamaica de Bowen

She called for Maggie to take the letter and post it,
then she began to fold her clothes for the trunk. Her
first thought was to leave the house secretly, but that of
course was impossible. Her trunk was in a basement
storage room off the kitchen to which Mrs. Renfrew
had the key. Then, of course, she would need the gig to
go to the village and book her passage on a hackney.
The simple act of leaving took more organization than
she felt capable of.

She sat down helplessly on her bed, feeling for the
first time in her life that she was utterly beyond coping
with the simplest arrangements. In a painful moment of
clarity, she saw that this was how her mother must feel
most of the time.

Total exhaustion overcame her and when she next looked up it was early morning. She had slept fully clothed and felt rather dreadful; her eyes were heavy from last night's weeping but her head was a little clearer.

She put on a robe, then sat up in bed reviewing the situation as she waited for the maid to bring her wash water.

What had she been thinking of yesterday? Of course she would not steal out of the house like a thief in the night. She would explain to the children first that—she thought fast—yes, that her aunt was poorly and she had been called to London; that in view of the summons, she was giving her notice and they would shortly be having a new governess; in the meantime, there would be another brief respite from studies. The story would serve. It would be easy to satisfy the children, although not easy to leave them, she realized.

As for Greville, she would not give him the satisfaction of thinking she was too ashamed to face him; no mousy little notes to him and no softening excuses, either. She would face him calmly and tell him she was leaving because he had made it impossible for her to keep this post a moment longer. In fact, she would not spend another night in this house, she decided. She would make her arrangements this morning and have one of the men drive her to the village. She would stay at the inn until she could get a passage to London.

The sunny east room where they breakfasted seemed less sunny today. As Jamaica took her seat opposite Mrs. Renfrew, she was stricken by the children's bright morning faces, so eager to begin their favorite day. It was Saturday, the day of picnics and boat rides and climbing the tall trees in the park.

With effort she put on a smile. "Good morning, children. I have some news to tell."

"Have we had a letter from mama?" Richard asked, wiping away a chocolate mustache as he set down his cup.

"The serviette, Richard, not your hand, please," she said automatically.

Three pairs of eyes turned toward her in anticipation while Mrs. Renfrew, at the end of the table, buttered her scone and pretended not to listen.

"What is it, what is it?" Sarah asked impatiently.

She smiled a little too brightly. "Well, it's rather sad news, for me at least. But I should think it is rather good news for you. You are to have another holiday."

"I say!" Richard said, looking very impressed.

"Why is it sad for you, Miss Jamie?" Caroline asked. "Shall you not have a holiday, too?"

"No, my pet. There is a poor sick lady in London, who is my aunt, and she is so ill that she has sent for me to take care of her."

"I'm sorry to hear that, Miss Jamie," Sarah said politely.

"How long shall you be gone?" Richard said, and she guessed that his mind was on the exact length of the holiday.

She took a deep breath. "Too long, I think, for me to take a leave of absence. I'm afraid I shall have to give notice."

"What's notice?" Caroline asked.

"Hush, Carrie," Sarah said. "It means she's going to leave us for good."

Caroline dropped her porridge spoon with a clatter. "No!" She ran from the table to Jamaica's side and clutched her. "It doesn't mean that!"

"Now, Carrie, you're making it very hard for me." Jamaica held her tightly. "I don't want to leave you. But it is all going to work out splendidly. I'm sure you will get a very nice new governess, and she probably won't work you nearly as hard as I do. And," she finished weakly, "I shall come and visit you often." Over Caroline's shoulder she looked pleadingly at Mrs. Renfrew for help.

Mrs. Renfrew came to the rescue. "Come, dears," she said, "eat up now, because you have a busy day. Jobe has to go down to Horsely and pick up his niece; she's going to be our new scullery maid. He's going down by boat and you can all go, too. He'll need some extra crew if he gets tired. It's almost five miles down river. And there's a fair at Horsely. If you help Jobe, I think Lord Dorrington will give you each a shilling to spend at the fair. And there'll be a picnic basket for dinner."

Jamaica looked up gratefully as Caroline climbed down from her lap and obediently returned to her chair. But the child had no appetite to finish her breakfast. "When are you leaving, Miss Jamie?"

"I don't know yet," she said, and disguised a sob by pretending to sneeze. "I'll tell you later, when you get back from Horsely. I must run along now; there's a lot to be done."

She left the room consoled only by the thought that she would be gone before the children returned, and she would not have to face the goodbyes. She willed herself to stay calm; she must appear composed and dignified when she faced Greville. At the thought of him, a furious rage swept through her, and she was glad. She would rather face him angry than drowning in tears.

As she climbed the kitchen stairs, she inquired of the

butler and was told that his lordship was in his study next to the book room.

She knocked and entered without waiting for permission. He sat behind a heavy rosewood desk. He wore spectacles and slid them down his nose to look over them as she entered. They softened his face somewhat, she noted, and made it look almost human.

"Excuse me, sir. I have come to give notice. I am leaving as soon as I have packed my things. If you would be so kind as to allow one of the stable staff to drive me to the village, I shall be out of here before sunset."

He removed his glasses with an irritated gesture. "Notice? Before sunset is hardly notice, Miss de Bowen. Six weeks is notice. Even two weeks is notice, for leaving a governess post."

"In regular circumstances, yes. I suppose it is. But you surely realize it is quite impossible for me to spend another night in this house."

He rubbed his eyes wearily and gestured to the chair beside his desk. Jamaica remained standing.

"I suppose you plan to stay at the inn until you can get a passage?"

"Precisely."

"There won't be another hackney until Monday. I don't see why you couldn't stay here."

"But I do."

He sighed, letting her know that she was an unnecessary complication in his already overburdened day. "I shall have quite a time finding a new governess, you know."

"There is no urgency, sir. It is summertime. Lessons need not begin in earnest until September."

He picked up his quill, then threw it down impatiently. "Huh! You've been drilling Richard like a sergeant major for his Winchester entrance, and suddenly there is no urgency?"

She stood silent, head up, a little surprised that he should even be aware of Richard's school plans.

"Not very conscientious, are you? Where, suddenly, is all your tender concern for poor little Caroline? You are quite made up to walking out of here in your pique and leaving her abandoned—to the tender mercies of her odious father!"

"Odious you may be, Lord Dorrington, but I am reasonably sure you would not so far forget yourself as to do the child a mischief. There are twenty servants here, all fond of the child. Mrs. Renfrew is a motherly soul, and Jobe would never let her come to harm. She will survive."

"But you won't if you stay another moment? Is that it?"

Steadfastly avoiding his eyes, she looked over his head at the forsythia bushes outside the window.

"Legally, you know, I could insist on three weeks' notice."

She glued her eyes to the forsythia buds. "I have a little more than three weeks' salary due. Legally, it will serve in lieu of notice. I insist that you keep it."

He gave a humorless laugh and fell to drumming his fingers on the polished surface of the desk with steady insistence. The sound drew her eyes down to the impatient left hand, the movement of the fingers. She was fascinated by it and could not look away until he stopped and spoke abruptly.

"I suppose it wouldn't help if I apologized. You did ask for it, you know."

"Yes, I did. And no, it wouldn't," she said stiffly.

He slapped the desk with both hands and pushed back in his chair, stretching out his legs. "Look, this is all too silly. Your main objection to working through your notice is having to spend another night under this roof with me, I take it. Then you shan't. I was leaving for London in the morning anyway, and I shall be gone the better part of a month. I shall spend tonight at the inn myself, and then you shan't have my presence polluting the air about you." He spoke as if he were humoring a child. He drew his chair back to the desk and took up his quill and writing paper.

"There is no need for you to put yourself to any inconvenience."

"No," he said, writing. "You are doing that quite nicely for me." He looked up quickly, then down again, continuing to write. "I shall place this advertisement for a governess in the Derbyshire *Gazette*. It will appear on Monday. If you will be gracious enough to interview the respondents and find your replacement, you shall be paid for the full month of June, and I shall be most obliged to you."

He threw down the quill. "Will you do that much?"

"Very well, sir," she said coldly and left the room.

If she had ever entertained the slightest suspicion that perhaps she had judged him harshly, that suspicion now vanished for good. He was, without question, the most odious creature she had ever come across, with about as much capacity for human feeling as a ginning mill. He did not give a fig about the children's welfare, and least of all did he care about her feelings. His only concern was his inconvenience if she left before a replacement was found. She had agreed to stay only because a smooth transition of tenure was more desirable for the children. He would, after all, be gone from the house.

But it would be so much harder on her to see the children day after day, knowing that she would finally have to make her farewells. She had not thought of it at the time, or she would probably have refused. It was done now; all that remained was the waiting through the days until there were some replies to the advertisement.

The following Tuesday applicants started to arrive. Greville, who had never hired a governess before, had not thought to request a letter, but had merely ended the notice with the address of Foxspur Park and the words, Apply In Person, Bringing References.

Nineteen women of various backgrounds, ages and qualifications kept Jamaica busy interviewing for ten days. By that time, she knew she had found a pleasant and likely candidate.

Grace Talbert was a quiet, well-read girl, the daughter of a minister. She had a little experience; three years with a Leicester family replacing a governess of failing health. She had stayed, she said, until the youngest boy was off to school, and she mentioned the name of a boys' school in Derby. Mrs. Renfrew assured her it was a decent enough school popular with the sons of the local gentry. The girl, then, could teach satisfactorily. She was twenty, but the shy befreckled face made her look like a child, and beneath the freckles lurked an unmistakable sense of fun. When Jamaica introduced her to the children she could see they would get along, although they were currently a trifle subdued at the thought of the change.

Jamaica sent a letter of inquiry to Miss Talbert's former employers, Sir Thomas and Lady Frimshaw, and waited to receive a satisfactory response; when it was in her hands, her task would be over. The inquiry was in the post by Friday morning; she could reasonably expect a reply early the following week. Mrs. Renfrew would make arrangements for Miss Talbert to move in, and Jamaica could be gone before Greville returned.

She knew there was no need to wait for the reply. Intuitively she trusted Miss Talbert, and even if she did not please Greville, she had kept the names, addresses and resumés of the other eighteen candidates. She could leave now without causing undue hardship, but she stayed to complete the bargain she had made.

CHAPTER TWELVE

DURING HER LAST DAYS AT FOXSPUR PARK Jamaica grew oddly tranquil. The demanding activity of sifting through various personalities to find her successor proved salutary, she supposed. She felt brisk, purposeful and completely detached.

While she waited for a reply from the Frimshaws, she packed her clothes carefully, put papers and schoolbooks in order and left meticulous notes for Miss Talbert so that the girl could pick up her duties with ease.

She had no heart for holding daily classes. Through her steady application, Richard was as ready as he would ever be for the September entrance examination, and her conscience was at rest. The children had found playmates of like age among the children of the village and the household staff; Jamaica saw no harm in this and allowed them to play together to their hearts' content. Mrs. Renfrew was now more or less in charge of their activities, and lenient as the lady was, they were all having a splendid boisterous time.

It had occurred to Jamaica that in midsummer, the Frinshaws might well be away from home, and that the reply to her inquiry would thereby be much delayed. She gave herself a time limit of ten days. If she had not received a reply by then, she would depart. Mrs. Renfrew was well briefed and would know what to do. Her decision would allow her to leave Foxspur Park well before Greville returned, and as long as she made up her mind that he was excised both from her heart and her experience, she found it easy to remain calm and rational.

When a letter arrived for Jamaica in the middle of the week, it was not the reply she was expecting from the Frimshaws. It was from Aunt Kate.

Two days later, as she reread the letter in the London-bound hackney, she marveled at how coolly she digested the news. Purged of emotion, everything was etched in crystal clarity now. Aunt Kate had, of course, not received her last letter. In her distress she had unthinkingly sent it to Waverly Terrace when she should have known that the family had long since returned to Devon. It was obvious as she read that Aunt Kate had never received her letter from Foxspur.

I will not beat about the bush, my dear. The news is mostly bad. The cargo of the *Golden Alice* is lost. A fire broke out while the vessel was docked putting on food and water. Canwood's notes are due at the end of this month. Regretfully, I must call you to your promise to plead pressing family business and leave immediately, which indeed will be no falsehood.

There is, however, a brighter side to all this, and that is the fact that I have found what I believe will be an infinitely desirable alternative to Lord Clare. We shall discuss it as soon as we meet. I am making arrangements to return to Waverly Terrace immediately, and I will await your arrival there. It should take you no more than three days to get there. You must make your plans to leave immediately upon receipt of this note. I know I need not emphasize to you the dire need for haste.

Your affectionate aunt, etc.

Post script. It has come to my attention that you have been seen riding in Hyde Park with the notorious Andrew MacFarland, now viscount of Kilgallen. When I told you to cast a speculative eye, I did not mean upon wastrels and Don Juans. Now I learn from your mama that you made his acquaintance in Paignton and that she actually encouraged it. How she could have been so empty-headed not to know of him and not to have at least taken the precaution of referring the matter to me, I cannot imagine. But the damage is done, and we must concentrate on getting you married before it becomes general knowledge. Gossip tends to die down after the season, and one must hope that Prinny does something sufficiently outrageous to make all other scandal pale—as he can usually be relied upon to do.

Jamaica folded the letter carefully, replaced it in her reticule and smiled at the lady with two little boys who sat facing her in the carriage. Now that the very worst had happened, strangely, it did not seem so bad after all. There was even an alternative to the marquis of Clare, it seemed; and even if the alternative came to naught, she believed that she had already suffered the worst that could happen to a woman. She had been betrayed, duped, humiliated. Andrew was not only the philanderer she had at first suspected, but one of great notoriety.

She had been foolish and ignorant, she realized, to go to such lengths to avoid matrimony. It was the single

state, not the wedded, that should be avoided at all
costs. The single state made a woman vulnerable; there
was no freedom in it, just dreadful possibilities. Marriage to the old gentleman could hardly be worse than
being single and employed by Greville.

She leaned back and closed her eyes, feeling fatalistic.
She was prepared to be putty in her aunt's hands and
meekly let her future overtake her.

The following afternoon found her in the duchess's
powder-blue boudoir at Waverly Terrace. Aunt Kate
was seated on a high-backed chair, her feet elevated on a
blue silk footstool piled high with cushions.

"Come give your aunt a kiss." The duchess held out
her arms and enclosed her niece. "Well! You look as
lovely as ever, I'm pleased to see."

Jamaica seated herself on the edge of a chaise longue
while her aunt examined her through the eye glass.

"A trifle pale, perhaps. But then it's been a trying
time for you, I'm sure."

She shrugged. "I am here to do your bidding, aunt.
And I won't cry about it, I promise you."

"Put it here, Cora." The duchess pointed to the small
gate-leg table as Cora entered with a tea tray. She nodded to her niece approvingly. "You're a good child,
Jamaica. At least that is one care off my shoulders.
Jouncing back and forth on the London turnpikes is not
a fitting occupation for my age."

Jamaica poured tea and handed her aunt a porcelain
cup and saucer. "Let's get down to business. You say
there is an alternative to the marquis of Clare?"

"Yes, it is quite providential. He is half the age of
Clare. Far more suitable. Some even consider him quite
handsome—in a rather serious way. He has an earldom,
a rather important one, and he is prepared to marry you

quite as soon as decent arrangements can be made. His need to settle down is almost as pressing as yours, having procrastinated for so long.''

Jamaica calmly sipped her tea. "Then simply name the time and the hour, Aunt Kate. What else remains to be done?''

The duchess put down her cup and raised her eyebrows. "Would you not care to know who he is, my dear? Marriage is a lifetime business, you know.''

"What possible difference can it make who he is? If I am ready to marry Lord Clare, then obviously I am ready to marry whomever you name. It must be quite evident that my heart is not engaged in this business. We are merely discussing a contract and the timely honoring of Mr. Canwood's notes. I should prefer to conclude the arrangement in that detached spirit.''

"My dear, it makes all the difference in the world.'' It saddened the duchess to see her niece so inured. "To marry Lord Clare is, mercifully, a very temporary arrangement. The man is well past sixty. But to marry a comparatively young man is to enter into an attachment of a far more permanent kind. Furthermore, we are discussing a man with whom you are slightly acquainted. I should think a modicum of curiosity would not be...amiss?''

Jamaica walked restlessly to the window, scarcely listening. She looked down at the sycamores fringing the lawns in the square below, then turned back into the room and poured herself a second cup of tea. "Not to mince words, of all the gossip-mongering, overbred monkeys I curtsied to when I came out last year, I cannot see that it signifies whether it be Lord This or Lord That. A young one will serve as well as an old one, if he can cover Canwood's notes.'' As she took up the cup to drink, she noted her aunt's saddened expression and gave her an encouraging smile. "But you are bent on telling me who it is, and since I shall have a new name, I might as well hear it now."

"It is Charles Greville, earl of Dorrington."

Jamaica jumped, spilling tea on her skirts, then brought the cup and saucer clattering down on the table with shaky hands.

She ran to her aunt, fell on her knees, and grasped the lady's hands so intently that she winced.

"Never!"

"What?" The duchess looked flabbergasted.

"I said never, aunt. Anyone in the world, but not Greville."

"My dear, how can you say that? I thought you would jump at the chance—any chance to escape Clare. And Greville! You have seen his property; he would be the most admirable of matches. You have had the opportunity of making his acquaintance, of observing him in his own home."

"Exactly, aunt. It is precisely because I have made his acquaintance that I come to you so ready to marry Lord Clare. I have suffered the very worst that can happen."

The duchess paled. "Dear God, he seduced you! And I thought I had only MacFarland to fear on that account."

"No, no, aunt. . .that, he did not do. But whatever may be done short of seduction, to torment and humiliate a woman. . .that he did."

"I had no idea you had taken such a dislike to him." She looked both relieved and bewildered.

"You would have, if you had received my letter. I wrote you that I was driven to leave my post because of his odious ways. But you had left for Camberleigh before the letter arrived."

"Never mind." The duchess recovered her composure. "Whatever in your girlish pride you may imagine to be his faults, I cannot, in good conscience, let you throw all this away so lightly. It is a marvelous piece of good fortune that you toss away with a word."

Jamaica's mind reeled as she groped for an explanation for this bizarre turn of events. Greville's words came back to her. *I have no idea who the lady shall be...so she be a good breeder...a friend of my late mother...I trust her judgment.* And it became appallingly clear.

"It was you he engaged to find him a wife?"

"Certainly it was I. It is high time he produced some heirs. The entire Greville family is on tenuous ground; he must do his duty."

Jamaica buried her face in her hands as the excruciating truth struck her with all its shameful implications. "Dear God, you knew! You knew about this when you brought the Grevilles to Paignton."

"Yes."

"And he? Did he know of it, too? And the Grevilles? And of course mama? Yes, of course. Everyone knew of it except me. What an idiot I am!"

"Stop it, Jamaica. Greville knew nothing of it, nor does he now. He came to Camberleigh the very day you left and begged me to find him a suitable wife. I agreed to do so. That is all. There is no need for this display."

Jamaica got to her feet now, trembling with anger. "So you conveniently had me engaged as a governess by the Grevilles in order to throw me in his path like a dropped handkerchief, for him to retrieve. It's monstrous! I have been nothing but a puppet with you pulling the strings. It's...it's unspeakable!"

"It is nothing of the sort," the duchess said sharply.

"I merely thought that if the two of you were thrown together by circumstances and nature took its course, as it is wont to do with two engaging people, it would be preferable to a match with Clare."

"I would rather die! It shall be the marquis of Clare. I insist. He at least has chosen me for myself. He at least is past the age of wanting to breed."

"One can never be sure of that, my dear. Are you quite made up to do this?"

"Nothing on earth could persuade me otherwise."

The duchess gave a long sigh. "I would never have thought you capable of such a foolish choice." After a long pause, she added, "Well, that's that. I shall send word to Arthur that you are here and he may call upon you."

"That won't be necessary, aunt. We can meet at the altar."

"Indeed it will be necessary. Poor Arthur has been waiting to hear whether you will have him these past twelve months. He will want to call upon you immediately to declare himself."

"I...I would rather simply meet him in church."

"I'm sure you would. But if you insist on going through with this ridiculous, unnecessary martyrdom, then you will wait upon his wishes, and he wishes to come to you personally and offer for you. He is at his house in Kent, and will probably be here within a day of receiving word."

"So be it," Jamaica said grimly.

After the message had been dispatched, Jamaica and her aunt settled into the most silent of waiting. Little conversation passed between them. Jamaica had the distinct feeling that her aunt was anxious to be gone, most uneasy at being in London in the off-season. They did no entertaining; there was no one left in town worth receiving.

At the duchess's invitation, a call was made by Madame Veronique, a costumier, who was engaged to measure Jamaica for a wedding gown. She was the best, the only Frenchwoman whose London business had survived the wars.

When asked whether she favored the empire style, still very popular for formal occasions, or the newer, longer-waisted styling, Jamaica merely shrugged.

"Whatever you think appropriate, *madame*. I am not in the least fussy; my aunt will confirm it."

The duchess took to her carriage every morning for a turn in the park, Jamaica refusing to leave the house. Daily she returned hoping to find her niece restored to her senses, but Jamaica's mind was made up to have Lord Clare, and thus to mope about the tall house like a condemned woman. The duchess was reduced to hoping that when Lord Clare arrived, Jamaica would have a last-minute change of heart and refuse his offer.

Such was not to be the case. Five days after the message was dispatched, the marquis arrived in London. A note delivered by his footman announced that he was in his house in Mayfair and would call on them at their earliest convenience.

"It can't be for supper, of course," the duchess said after reading the note, while Clare's footman waited discreetly by the door to carry back a reply. "You haven't a proper thing to wear in your luggage." She dropped her voice. "It would hardly do to remind him of your occupation over the past months. What do you say to inviting him this afternoon?" she asked Jamaica. "Say, an early tea, about three o'clock?"

"Whatever you please, aunt. It can't be too soon for me."

Arthur Sterling arrived promptly. His knee britches and coat were a somber gray, as befits a man of advanced years, but his waistcoat was a virulent lavender, as if to assure his prospective bride that he was not too far out of step, that he was aware of the newest fads of the young bloods.

After an extravagant bow to the ladies, he was hard put to straighten up again. Jamaica was obliged to support him, and she helped to seat him carefully in a chair.

"Miss de Bowen," he said, wheezing fitfully, "it is a great delight to see you again. As your aunt must have told you, I have thought of you often and fondly since we met last summer, and now—" He was obliged to stop and catch his breath.

"Lord Clare," the duchess put in, "if you will excuse me for a few minutes, I have some urgent business to attend to, as I believe you have with my niece." She rose purposefully and left the room.

Jamaica had attempted to numb all her senses and not form any visual impression of the man, but it was not possible. He was there, flesh and blood, before her eyes; and she could not in all civility keep them closed.

He was not, after all, as she remembered him. His nose was reddish rather than purple, and he was much smaller than she had imagined. His eyes were a washed-out blue, and the left one watered slightly. A sparse white mustache covered his upper lip, badly snuff stained, as were his thin nostrils. As he took his tea, she could hear the clack of ivory dentistry on the thin china cup.

He was a dabber, she noted, his kerchief constantly in

use so that he did not bother to sleeve it but fussed with the lace on it with his small white fingers. When he reached for his teacup on the side table, he would clasp the kerchief between his knees.

His face seemed shrunken under the disproportionate luxuriance of a full powdered wig. It was the kind she had seen in portraits of the last century, tied in a queue with a stiff black ribbon. In one who affected a lavender waist-coat, she could think of no good reason for the anachronism, except that he was covering a bald head. There were wigmakers aplenty who simulated the more abbreviated coiffures of today for bald pates; but perhaps Clare felt the outrageous style made him less a bald old man and more of a wag, in the manner of the pace-setting blades who took pride in sporting a bizarre item of dress. The actual effect was to make him look the more absurd.

A thin crack occurred in the stony stoicism she had managed to acquire over the past few weeks, but she ignored it.

He seemed to be preoccupied with his dabbing and wheezing, so that she began to despair of his ever speaking up. Finally, her patience wearing thin, she prompted him.

"Lord Clare, I believe you have done me the express honor of traveling up from Kent because you have something in particular to say. Please feel free to speak."

"Ah, yes. It is settled then?"

"I beg your pardon?"

"Shall I speak from here? Too much bother getting up."

"Yes, yes. Please do."

"Miss de Bowen, will you do me the honor of becoming my wife?"

"I will, and the honor is all mine," she said quickly.

"I think you should know," he said very solemnly, "that I am not as young as I look."

She was tormented with the desire to howl with laughter. She turned aside and fussed with a bowl of yellow roses, hiding her face from him, and when she was able she answered with great solemnity, "Age has never been of much consequence to me, sir."

"Then, my dear, we are both fortunate. I shall press your aunt to expedite the arrangements so that we may be wed and return to Kent together." Of a sudden he grasped the malacca cane that rested beside his chair and thumped on the carpet, calling out with a strength of voice he had not shown until now. "Standish!"

His man, Standish, entered the room immediately to help his lordship creak his way out, while Jamaica dipped in a deep ceremonial curtsy. At the door he turned back.

"I know the bishop of St. Margaret's. I shall have the marriage license before the end of the week. I shall expect to hear from your aunt before then. Good day."

CHAPTER THIRTEEN

JAMAICA FOUND HERSELF in complete agreement with the marquis of Clare; the sooner, the better. She did not know if her absolute purity of purpose could withstand the pressure of too many days. It was, she told herself, like marching into battle. It must be done on the spur of the moment and without thought. It did not do to ponder over the meaning of the act, the possible consequences. To tarry was to invite the courage to fail.

Aunt Kate was of a different mind. After stressing the need for haste to this point, she now swung about unaccountably. Suddenly nothing short of a full-fledged society wedding would do. She was adamant about it.

"No, no," she said after supper that evening, "it simply will not do to be unseemly in our haste. I have thought better of it. You shan't be married here at all. It is only fitting that you be married with dignity at Camberleigh."

"Camberleigh! But that will mean a monstrous delay. It can't be done by the end of the week."

"We have until the end of the month and we shall profit from it. I insist that your mama, that the entire family be present to witness the rites."

"Aunt Kate!" Jamaica said hotly, "you talk as if this were a celebration of joy. I do not in the least care to have the entire family witness this comedy. To watch me as I walk down the aisle with a doddering little man in a powdered wig? How could you?"

"Don't fret, my dear. I will take care of Arthur and see that he looks presentable. But as for holding the wedding here at St. Margaret's, absolutely not. It has an air of scandal about it. What with your unfortunate episode with that MacFarland fellow, we are obliged to put the lie to all rumors."

"There was no unfortunate episode with MacFarland, aunt. We were merely friends."

The duchess frowned. "That in itself is a rumor that must be scotched. I cannot imagine how the Grevilles could have allowed you to continue such a liaison under their very noses. How did you explain it to them?"

Jamaica narrowed her eyes knowingly at the duchess. In this time of crisis she had acquired a certain canniness, an insight into her aunt's manipulations. Now she fully understood Mrs. Greville's lenient attitude. "You know perfectly well how it happened. You have been in regular correspondence with Elizabeth Greville since I first came to London. She probably recounted my every move to you."

The duchess wrinkled her nose but kept her dignity. "And what if she did? How could you, Jamaica? How could you tell her he was an old family friend?"

Jamaica threw up her arms despairingly and began to pace the room like a caged lioness. "Oh, what does it signify now? Let us get this business over, for pity's sake."

"Quite, quite." The duchess seated herself at her writing table, removed a gold pencil and a tablet from the slender drawer and began to make some notes. "We shall expedite matters without appearing to do so. I shall talk to Arthur first thing in the morning and then return to Camberleigh. You shall stay here for your fittings. I shall have to leave you my abigail. You had better order some kind of trousseau from Madame Veronique in the morning, although it won't give her much time. She'll have to drop everything else. But it is *de rigueur*. This is hardly a runaway marriage, my dear. Your sister's wedding set a certain precedent.''

''But Kitty's wedding was not at Camberleigh!'' Jamaica protested, still pacing.

The duchess cast a reproachful look at her wayward niece. ''Kitty did not marry a marquis!''

''You are making this very trying for me, aunt. I really don't see the necessity for all the folderol.''

''It will only take a few more days than if we rushed into it as if we were averting an imminent scandal. Let us always remember that we are guardians of the good name of the family.'' She squared her shoulders with a military gesture. ''We cannot tarnish it by indecent haste. And we will not.''

''So you are bent on making a spectacle of me before all the world?''

The duchess gave a tolerant sigh. ''If that is how you choose to put it. . .yes. Now be so good as to ring the bell for Osgood.''

Jamaica recognized the adamantine position where further argument was useless. She went to the silk cord by the door of the drawing room and tugged so viciously that the tassel broke off in her hand. She muttered an expletive behind clenched teeth and threw the tassel across the room.

The duchess bent her head to the writing tablet and penned a brief note, studiously ignoring Jamaica's rage.

''Osgood,'' she said as the butler entered, ''have Chalmers prepare tne phaeton for returning to Devon in the morning. We shall start a little before nine. Tell Cora to pack my trunk tonight. My niece will be staying in here for a week or so, so I will not be closing down the house. And please have this note delivered to the marquis of Clare in Mayfair.''

"Very good, Your Grace," he said, taking the folded note from her hand and sealing it in the envelope she gave him.

"Oh, and have the bellpull repaired, will you," she added casually. "It must be rather frayed. It just fell off in my niece's hand."

LADY CAMBERLEIGH FELT DISTINCTLY ODD presenting herself at Arthur's Mayfair home before nine-thirty. It was hardly an hour for persons of quality to be stirring, let alone to be making calls. But a crisis called for strong measures, and she had sent word to Arthur the previous evening. He had responded very willingly to the unusual request. And well he might, she thought, as she was led up the broad swirl of staircase to the morning room on the second floor.

The morning room was quite oppressive. The heavy red velvet that draped the fine bow window was most unseasonable for July. But then Arthur never used the Mayfair house except in the winter. The stuffiness in the air informed her that the house had been closed up for months.

Arthur joined her from a side door as soon as she was seated. He was dressed in a splendid velvet morning robe, his head partially covered by a nightcap set at a rakish angle. It allowed a glimpse of thinning white hair, the skin beneath it a surprisingly healthy pink.

They sat together over cups of hot chocolate with the unstrained familiarity of old friends. Arthur's bronchial condition was at its most severe upon rising. He gave concentration to his breathing and spoke in brief elliptic comments.

"Seen bishop...marriage license Thursday next." He paused to recover and take a swallow of chocolate. "Can you have the girl ready by then?"

The duchess shuddered visibly. "Arthur, she is not a fowl to be dressed for the table."

The kerchief appeared from a deep pocket of the robe, and he dabbed his mustache with it. "I'm too old for niceties, Kate," he said, dismissing her excessive delicacy with a petulant wave of the kerchief.

"Quite. And you are too old for Jamaica."

Arthur's eyes grew beady with attention. "What'r 'ye saying, woman? Girl said she'd have me straight out."

"Yes, Arthur. But you know girls. Very often hasty in their decisions and regretting it later. My niece has been through a trying time lately. It's quite possible she doesn't know her own mind. You know how they can be."

"Balderdash. That one's not fickle. She can hardly wait." His mouth widened into a cunning grin, displaying expensively carved ivory teeth. "Standish told me what she said when he brought round my note. 'Can't be too soon for me,' she said. 'Can't be too soon.'"

The duchess pressed her lips together. "Be that as it may, I insist she have a week or so to think it over."

Arthur pouted like a child put unwillingly to bed. "But I don't want to lose another week."

"It won't be lost. I am returning to Camberleigh this morning, and I shall plunge immediately into the arrangements on the assumption that she will not falter in her decision."

"Camberleigh!" His voice became shrill. "It's to be here! St. Margaret's...this week!"

The duchess assumed a look of deep reproach. "Arthur," she said in sepulchral tones, "this is a de Bowen wedding...de Bowen and Sterling."

He listened carefully as Kate went on. "You know very well that the only proper setting for such a union is the de Bowen family seat. St. Margaret's indeed! Why not Gretna Green? I'm surprised at you."

If he felt in the least chastened, he disguised it well Finally he said, "The deuce take it, Kate. Do what you must, but be quick about it. I can't be rattling around this house for days on end. It's pesky noisy. Can't sleep. Carriages racketing around all hours of the night. Damned strawberry vendors piping up and down the street ungodly hours of the morning. It's purgatory here."

"Then you shan't tolerate it one more day. Do as I do. Take off this morning for Kent and wait there in comfort until I send word that it's time to come to Camberleigh."

"Dash it all! Did I come haring down to London just for this? Could have stayed home and spared meself the trouble. Not the only gel after me, y'know."

"Yes, I know. Therefore you will not be plunged into despair if she should change her mind."

"Breach of promise!" he squeaked.

"Nonsense. I am confident a Sterling would never allow his name to be dragged through the civil courts, and may I remind you that it was at your own insistence that you came to make a personal declaration to the girl. You said you did not care for proxies."

"Still, the whole thing's a damn waste of time, considering."

She smiled winsomely at him. "I'm sure a man of your spirit will easily make up for lost time on his wedding night."

She left him feeling moderately hopeful but prepared to lose, she thought. At this juncture she could do no more.

Chalmers jumped down from his perch as he saw the duchess emerge from the house. "We are not returning to Devon after all, Chalmers. Please drive to the Great North Road. We are bound for Derbyshire."

She settled back into the cushions for the long ride. From the gilt mirror facing her, she could tell that rising with the servants did nothing flattering for a woman of her years. She slipped out of the city shoes that pinched so abominably and set her swollen feet on the footrest, smoothing out her light gray alpaca traveling skirt.

How like Canwood to fail again. How dismally consistent he was. And of course he must bring things to a head at the height of the season.

She had been so sure her plan would carry without a hitch. Certainly she could never have imagined things coming to this. Kate de Bowen chasing up and down the county thoroughfares like a highwayman. Where had she gone wrong? Charles Greville was so uncannily like Henry de Bowen, Jamie's late father, the way she remembered him when Jamie was just a little thing. He was intelligent, masterful—so different from the Almack's types. He was neither a dandy nor a gossip. He was perfect for Jamaica, no question about it. Surely the girl felt some stirrings. Well, at least she wasn't indifferent to him. Far from it. That, at least, gave her hope.

And what was Charles about, she wondered? She couldn't imagine a man of his taste remaining indifferent to Jamaica. It was unthinkable. Of course, she was nothing like his late wife Stella, except that they were both beauties; but he had been young and foolish then, a mere boy. And he had learned a bitter lesson. As a mature man, surely he must recognize Jamaica as the perfect partner for him. True, he had looked upon her merely as hired help; he knew nothing of the subterfuge. But that wouldn't stop him. He had the same freewheeling independence as Henry, and was certainly quite capable of flouting social practice should he feel inclined. It was what made him so eminently suitable for Jamaica. . . .

Charles had licked his wounds quite long enough, she decided. It had taken him a full five years to acknowledge that he was bound to remarry. She had assumed that meeting Jamaica, seeing her regularly, would do the rest, that nature would take its course as surely as water finds its own level. Ah, well, they were both hardheaded and mightily independent. She would just have to try a little harder. She certainly wasn't going to give up.

For the space of the two-day journey, her mind wrestled ceaselessly with the puzzle. When they reached the very gates of Foxspur Park she was still struggling to resolve it.

When the phaeton rounded the last curve and the house came into view, the duchess breathed an involuntary sigh of pleasure. She had not visited Dorrington since old Countess Clara died. It cheered her to see the park grounds still looking the way Clara liked to see them; Charles had not let his mother's memory down. She tried to envisage Jamaica as mistress of all this. . . and her strength of purpose grew.

Mrs. Renfrew remembered her; she was received with deference, and the apologetic explanation that his lordship was in the stables, but was being informed immediately.

While she waited in a pleasant west-wing sitting room, she sipped some of Mrs. Posset's excellent black-berry cordial. The good woman had remembered her taste for it.

Greville burst in very shortly, looking slightly hot and disreputable. He gave a quick disparaging look down at his creased and dusty nankeens. "Forgive me, Lady Camberleigh. I did not want to keep you waiting while I changed. What a charming surprise." He bent over her hand and squeezed it affectionately, then pecked her cheek.

The duchess caught a not unpleasant whiff of the stable and edged back in her chair. "Well...yes, Charles. As you may guess, I haven't covered the inter-minable Great North and arrived unannounced for the sake of a pleasure jaunt. I do have business of some urgency. But it can wait at least until you are bathed and suitably dressed, my dear." The reproach in her voice was most affectionate. "I can tell the single life finds you somewhat remiss in the social graces."

Greville smiled. "Quite right, Aunt Kate," he said, unconsciously slipping back into the form of address he had used as a child, "I look dreadful and smell worse. And I'm sure you would like to rest and refresh your-self. I'll have your trunk sent up, and Mrs. Renfrew shall prepare you a room. Shall we meet here for sherry?" He glanced at his muddy fob watch and cleaned off the dial with his shirt sleeve to determine the time. "Say, half-past six?"

"Seven," she replied, still not knowing how she would tackle the meeting.

At seven Greville was much improved; he was freshly shaven, dressed for dinner, and he smelled faintly of some pleasant talcum powder.

He chose to serve the sherry himself. "I am most honored, Lady Camberleigh, that you come all this way to call."

"I have found you a wife, Charles," she replied. "Nothing short of that would have brought me."

"I thought as much. But I didn't dream you would make the journey yourself. A word from you, and I would have waited upon you in Devon."

"You know how I detest traveling, but this is an extraordinary match. My coming here in person only emphasizes the unique nature of the affair."

He smiled, pleasantly enough, waiting for her to go on.

"Are you not going to ask me who it is?"

"Are you not going to tell me, regardless?" he teased.

"I expect a little flutter of curiosity, Charles. A little importuning. It's a wife we are discussing. Your wife; the mother of your children."

"My dear duchess, surely you realized when I threw myself on your mercy last summer that it was a matter of expediency. I must perpetuate this house and, not least, quiet my noisy relatives. Elizabeth in particular gives me no peace on the subject. But there's no flutter about it. I simply have every confidence in your judgment."

It was too trying for words. How alike they were: two stubborn idiots of superior intelligence, both bent on making their lives all business and no pleasure. If she were to knock their two silly heads together, she wondered which would crack.

"The gel's my niece, and curious or not, you may as well know straight off that she is young, absolutely charming, and will make you the envy of every man this side of the Thames."

He looked puzzled. "Your niece? I thought you married her off last spring."

"That was Kitty, the other niece. Henry had two daughters."

"Yes, I vaguely remember that," he said in a lukewarm voice. "Is she old enough to know what she is doing?"

"She's rising twenty. Of course she's old enough."

He looked shrewdly into her eyes. "Then she must have come out. It's a wonder to me she wasn't snapped up in her first season if she's such a charmer."

"She turned down all offers. She doesn't care for dandies." She took a long, appraising look at him as he sat leaning forward, his chin resting on one fist. He was a very fine figure of a man. "She's rather fickle—as a first-class beauty has a right to be," she added defiantly.

"But not too fickle for a blind match."

She noted the dry tone of voice. "Ah, but it won't be a blind match, Charles." She was improvising desperately now. "You'll have to woo her and win her."

Greville reached for his sherry and sipped it slowly before he answered. "I've had my fill of beauties, Lady Camberleigh. I have no desire to enter the lists to win a prize. I thought I made it very clear. It is why I suggested that a plain girl would serve very well." He shook his head. "I'm sorry if you misunderstood. You have put yourself to a deal of unnecessary trouble." He stood up and held out his arm to her.

"Come, I'll try to make amends. Mrs. Posset has prepared a most excellent supper for us."

At the supper table, she munched dolefully on a superb galantine of chicken, as if chewing over her mistakes. So far she had handled things very clumsily, but there must be a way to salvage it.

She did not return to the subject until the meal was almost over and an elaborate sherry trifle was placed before them. She was fond of all the Grevilles, looked upon them almost as family. Her friendship with Clara dated back to early childhood. She realized now that she should have been more open with Charles.

"The thing of it is, Charles," she began, "my niece has a very reckless stepfather who has put a dent in the family fortune. The poor girl has to take it upon herself to bail them all out by marrying quickly and well. She is currently at Waverly Terrace, preparing to marry the marquis of Clare."

"Old Clare, eh?" He cocked an appreciative eyebrow. "Well, that should certainly do it."

"Of course. But you could do it, too, Charles. It hurts me to see her throw herself away on him when she could have you."

He shook his head firmly. "No, I mean it. I'm not in the wooing business."

"Whatever has happened to you, Charles? You can scarcely consider Arthur Sterling as serious competition. It would be the simplest of things." She paused, then asked very softly, "It's not the money, is it?"

"No." The lean serious face took on a dark warm tint. "I'm afraid I've been less than completely frank, Lady Camberleigh. Since last summer when I called upon you to find me a wife, I have—" he stopped, then began again awkwardly "—I...my feelings have been more than a little engaged by a gov—a lady. I never expected it to happen again, you see."

The duchess saw very well. She nodded sympathetically. "I quite understand. And you hesitated to come out with it because you wanted to spare my feelings." She sighed tolerantly. "You would have spared me more if you'd saved me the journey." She leaned across the table and patted his hand. "Never mind. Go after her, Charles. You have no further need of my services."

"No, no, you don't understand. There are difficulties, you see. It's impossible. First, she was employed as a governess to the children and . . . ." He shrugged.

"What poppycock is this, Charles? Don't tell me that would stop you. It would never have stopped Henry de Bowen, and you and he were cut from the same cloth. If you've a mind to do it, you'll do it with panache, and you'll make it proper." Having made short shrift of his first objection, she leaned forward intently. "What else?"

His expression became rather hangdog. "What else is this, Lady Camberleigh: I cannot think of one good reason she would have me. She left here in a huff only last week. I behaved very badly." He closed his eyes briefly as if trying to erase an excruciating memory. "No, it's out of the question. I think she would sooner face me carved up on a platter for dinner than receive an offer from me. I am persona non grata with a vengeance."

"Poor girl. You must have been quite dreadful—if you really believe you have earned her contempt. You probably deserve it," she finished tartly.

"I do."

It was a painful subject to him, and he could not fathom why the duchess was, of a sudden, very sanguine. She was wreathed in smiles, as if she truly enjoyed his distress.

She folded her serviette and rising sprightfully from the table spoke very cheerfully. "Not to worry, Charles. You know what they say about the course of true love. I suggest you have a good night's sleep; I certainly need one. I must start out for Camberleigh early tomorrow. We'll have a little chat over breakfast. I know you'll feel better then. After all, you could hardly feel worse. It is written all over your face.''

Greville retired in the same disconsolate mood he had suffered for many days. The duchess went to her bed in a state of exhilaration and drifted into a sequence of quite satisfactory dreams.

LADY CAMBERLEIGH NEVER TOOK BREAKFAST. The following morning in the breakfast room, she seated herself in a chair from which she could best see the rose bed, although the blooms were not such fine specimens as her own. She worked her way heartily through a dish of scrambled eggs, two muffins with marmalade and two cups of coffee. She was on the second cup before Greville entered, squinting painfully at the golden sunlight that fell on one-half of the table. He seated himself opposite the duchess, his back to the glorious morning.

''I'm late. I apologize. I had a very restless night.''

She regarded the dark smudges under his eyes and smiled angelically. ''So you did, poor boy. I slept like a log.''

He poured some coffee and sat drinking it wearily, while she took up her lorgnette and glanced at the morning newspaper. ''I see you still have the most splendid horse fairs in Derby. I do wish I had time to go over there, but I really must start for home. Houseguests coming, don't you know?''

She looked up from the paper, then pointedly down at his place at the table. It was empty except for the coffee cup. ''Are you not going to serve yourself, Charles? If you didn't sleep you should at least fortify yourself with something better than that.''

He shook his head.

She began to enjoy herself. "But there are grilled kippers on the sideboard. The scrambled eggs are quite delicious. What about some muffins, straight from the oven? Mrs. Posset is excellent with oranges. I must have her send her marmalade recipe to my cook."

"Really, Lady Camberleigh, I'm not hungry this morning."

"Well, in that case," she said, setting the newspaper down, "I believe we should have our final talk."

He put down his cup and stared into it morosely. "What else is there to say?"

"I say you should follow your heart. Any fool could tell you that. Always assuming, of course, that this governess is a lady. That is to say—" she paused, pondering, "—as long as she is not common. She doesn't have to be highborn. If she's intelligent enough to teach children, she'll probably bring it off quite well, all things considered."

"I'm afraid it's beyond retrieving. I really did make myself anathema to her. If I begged for forgiveness and groveled she wouldn't soften."

"Probably not, Charles. My advice is to take her by storm. Leave the groveling until later."

His mouth formed an ironic half smile. "Dear lady, you do not know her as I do."

"Quite true. Tell me a little about her."

He sighed, as if it were a futile exercise, but he was obliged out of courtesy to humor his guest. "Where to begin? Miss de Bowen is forthright, clever and quite as stubborn as—"

He stopped in reaction to a gasp of shock across the table.

"Miss who?"

"Miss de—" He stopped again, his face paling to a light shade of gray, then with no sound at all issuing from his lips, he formed the words again. "Miss de Bowen."

The duchess was enraptured as she watched the play of emotions. His face became a pantomime expressing horror, disbelief, an infinite variety of sentiments, while his color ebbed and flowed, ranging from palest parchment to deep burgundy.

At length he muttered something unintelligible, and was obliged to clear his throat several times before he could make himself understandable. At last his words came out in a hoarse rasp. "Not your niece, Lady Camberleigh?"

"The very same. I should have thought you too clever not to have put two and two together before now."

"Oh, my dear, you have no idea how thoroughly stupid I can be." His voice was still no more than a rasp.

"Oh, yes, I do!"

He shook his head as if he had been dreaming. "Never in a million years would I have taken her for a Camberleigh de Bowen."

She poured the stricken man some more coffee. "I don't see why not. She is quite typical, you know."

His eyes were glassy with astonishment. "How could I have guessed that your niece would be in a post teaching someone's children?"

"There is that, of course," she conceded. "I confess it does appear highly improbable. But there it is! Now what are you going to do about it?"

"Pray that you will find it in your heart to forgive my offensiveness to your niece."

"No, no. I mean what are you going to do about winning her hand?"

He looked at her in confusion. "It really doesn't alter things. She still won't have me; now I know she's your niece I'm more convinced than ever."

"I am quite sure she will have you, and I know her well. Where are your brains, man? Have you locked them away with your spunk? All she needs is to be swept away by a man who shows himself to be in absolute control. Are you at all capable of doing that, Charles? After all these years?"

His eyes seemed to flame just for a moment. "Of course! If only I thought there was half a chance."

"Then for God's sake get yourself together and do it before it's too late. The only chance you have is now, before she ties herself up with Lord Clare."

He shot up from the table and was halfway to the door when she called him back. He turned, gripping the door jamb like a horse chafing at the bit.

That's more like it, she thought. "She's at Waverly Terrace for her gown fittings. There's to be no groveling, mind; no bended knee. She'll give you a fierce argument no doubt, but don't take no for an answer. She needs a firm hand."

As he raced back into the room and hugged her, she almost added, *Compromise her first if you have to and leave the explanations till later,* but instead she whispered, "Good luck."

The next instant he was gone. She had a week, traveling back to the West Country, to wonder if she had done the right thing. She could only pray that she had.

CHAPTER FOURTEEN

ARTHUR STERLING, MARQUIS OF CLARE, sat in his sitting room with the London *Times* on his knees, but his thoughts were elsewhere.

The old duck was two days' ride from London, halfway back to Camberleigh by now. And the girl was just around the corner, so to speak.

He had not turned back for Kent that morning as she had suggested. Kate was up to something nefarious; there was no doubt in his mind. Months ago she had told him he might have a sporting chance with her niece if he waited until July, and for months he had put aside the thought of all other women in favor of the de Bowen girl. Just when it was all going along beautifully and he could congratulate himself on the win, suddenly Kate was balking. Time was a costly investment at his age; the moment had come to cash in. It was now, while Kate was out of touch and the delicious young thing over at Waverly Terrace had a mind to it. The bishop at least was good as his word. His clerk had delivered the marriage license an hour ago. Why wait another moment? He chuckled to himself. If Kate could be sly, so could he.

"Standish," he called out, "See that my tan silk britches are pressed. I'm going calling before dinner."

"MY DEAR MADEMOISELLE, this is terrible," Madame Veronique murmured through a mouthful of pins.

The elegant little couturiere crouched on the blue carpet scowling at the loose folds of the gown. She looked into the full-length pier glass and gave a Gallic shrug to the reflection of the tall listless girl who seemed to be melting away.

"Two times I take the measure. Two times I refit you. And still it fits like a sack!" She narrowed her eyes accusingly at the face in the mirror. "You are not going to get any thinner, are you?"

The girl gave a heavy sigh. "It doesn't matter, *madame*. Just leave it the way it is."

"What a suggestion!" Madame dropped the pins in shock. "This is your wedding gown, and I am Madame Veronique. You think I could leave it like this! It would be all over London in a week. You and I would be the laughingstock, *mademoiselle*; the laughingstock!"

"Don't concern yourself. The wedding is not to be in London; it is to be far away, in Devon. It will not signify." Jamaica turned from the mirror, the gown drooping and dragging, and walked across the room to sit on her bed while the seamstress chased after her on her knees.

"Yes, yes, and your aunt plans a very complete guest list. She wants everything *comme il faut*. You stand up in a potato sack on the most important day of your life—and you think it will not be 'eard in London? Bad news, it travels faster than a post 'orse." She got to her feet, and wheedling, held out an arm to the girl slumped on the bed. "Come, *mademoiselle*, if you please. Stand up and let me see what I can do. Such a slender waist. It would be a crime."

The girl rose reluctantly and took up her post again before the mirror.

The gown was a soft, subtle turquoise in watered silk. Since the bride had been able to suggest no color preference at all, *madame* had thought it best to bring out the color of her eyes. It had been a good choice, but *madame* was disturbed. She had seen disinterested brides before, of course. The marriage of convenience constituted perhaps one-half of her business—but this girl—it seemed she wasn't eating at all. She was losing inches faster than her seamstresses could sew. It was like a race, she thought grimly, to get the girl costumed and to the church before she disappeared altogether.

And then there was the trousseau. She had not even started on it. What would she do about that? Lady Camberleigh had left very clear instructions that the girl was to have a complete trousseau wardrobe according to her personal taste. But the girl refused to suggest anything. Her taste was apparently nonexistent. The nightgowns? "Whatever you think, *madame*." The traveling costumes? "As you wish, *madame*." The tea gowns? "If you must, *madame*." She was a block of wood, this bride; more like a stick.

Madame Veronique worked furiously with her pins, smoothing the silk over waist and hips snugly, the carefully finished seams disappearing behind the new chalk marks.

"*Voilà!*" She got to her feet once more and took a final critical look all around to satisfy herself. Carefully she undid the tiny pearl buttons at the back and helped the poor thing out of the dress.

In her petticoats the girl went to the armoire and took out the first thing to hand, a plain, dun-colored calico. Very dowdy, very out of style. *Madame* rolled her eyes. Such a lovely creature, and about to become a marchioness. She dressed like a London governess left behind in high summer. In the fashion business there was nothing you did not see. Nothing!

She decided she must have the final word on the trousseau, and she took a deep breath. "*Mademoiselle*, since you wish me to make the decisions, I should tell you that the complete trousseau for a lady of quality will include night things, dressing gowns, morning gowns, tea gowns, traveling wear and ball dresses—which in summer will include garden-party attire—and of course 'ats. But you will see your milliner about that. I shall design two of everything, and I shall favor greens and turquoise trim. But it will be basically white—your coloring was made to be set off with white." She stopped, noting the girl's pallor this morning. "I must warn you, you will need to apply some color to your face or you will disappear into the white. You are too pale."

The girl nodded her head meekly then sighed. "I used to be very tanned when I lived in the West Country."

"Tanned!" *Madame* was shocked. "Then it is better you live there no more. We can't 'ave you looking like a farm girl. At least with rouge you can control the amount and the quality of the color."

She smoothed out the turquoise silk, now bristling with pins and folded it carefully into a large square of ecru linen, then draped it gingerly over her forearm.

"I shall be back on Saturday morning. Meanwhile, at least try to eat a good dinner every day, then God willing, you will not change shape again."

She swept out of the room, muttering under her breath, "Tanned indeed—*quel horreur*," and rueing the price she had quoted the duchess.

JAMAICA STARED AT HERSELF in the mirror after the
costumier left, wondering exactly what it was she felt.
Aunt Kate was two days gone, and still she had not
stepped foot outside the house at Waverly Terrace. She
was neither happy nor unhappy. She tried hard to recall
what it was like to feel either state, and she could not.
She wondered vaguely if it was something to do with being confined here for so long, and if prisoners felt this
way after a while. But of course she wasn't a prisoner.
There was nothing stopping her from going out. She
simply had no desire to do so; no desire to read, to walk,
to ride in the park. It seemed her only activity was
standing up and turning around for Madame Veronique. And the woman constantly plagued her with
questions she had no answer for. She simply couldn't be
bothered to think at all.

Cora, Aunt Kate's abigail, had taken the hint that she
wanted no company, no diversions. She went quietly
about her business, neither approving nor disapproving,
and keeping out of Jamaica's way. She was discreet and
well trained, as all Aunt Kate's staff were.

In a half hour she knew the dinner bell would sound,
and she would obediently leave her room, walk down
one flight of stairs to the dining room, sit alone at the
mahogany table with its lace cloth, and push the food
around for the duration of three courses.

Until then she would lie back on her bed and once
more examine the decorative plaster work on the ceiling.
There were precisely twenty-four corniced sections to
the design. Each alternate section had a cornucopia, and
at first she thought they were identical; now she
discovered that the number of grapes in each bunch
varied.

Cora disrupted her study by entering to announce a

visitor...her first visitor since she arrived at Waverly Terrace. The calling card belonged to Lord Clare. He was her betrothed, she reasoned impersonally, and as such, it was only fitting that she should receive him. Cora became tedious for the first time, and insisted on dressing her in something freshly laundered and fussing with her hair.

In little more than fifteen minutes, she entered the sitting room. She was greeted by the ludicrous powdered wig again as the marquis bent to take her hand.

"How good of you to call, Lord Clare," Jamaica said tonelessly. "Please be seated."

He appeared more vigorous today than the first time he called, and with the aid of his cane, was able to straighten up, wait for Jamaica to seat herself and then place himself in a tall-backed armchair close to hers.

After a few inanities about the weather, he became limber enough to cross his legs. He took out his kerchief and rested it atop his knee.

"Ever since Lady Camberleigh informed me that you might be willing to entertain a proposal, I have cast aside all other prospects. And I have waited with impatience for your aunt to send word that the moment had come."

Jamaica sat with her eyes glued to the kerchief adorning his knee, amazed that he managed to leave it there undisturbed for so long.

"Do you know how long it has been, Miss de Bowen?"

She stared at him startled. Was he alluding to the kerchief? It must be at least a minute—a minute and a half? She collected her wits and tried to recall what he had just said—something about waiting to propose.

"I beg your pardon, Lord Clare?"

"It has been almost a year," he replied. "Perhaps not such a long time for one of your age, but I should point out that I am more mature than you."

"Yes, quite." She applied herself to the task of concentrating.

"A week ago, when the word finally came, I prepared myself immediately, and at considerable effort and expense, came straightway to London and announced my presence."

"You did indeed, sir."

"Then Tuesday last, your aunt called upon me before starting her journey home, to announce that the wedding was to be a large planned affair held in Camberleigh."

Jamaica fell to counting the buttons on his silk britches, then remembered she was to pay attention.

"Yes, yes. Aunt Kate assured me that it will only take a few more days."

"Miss de Bowen, have you any idea how long it takes to bring about a wedding such as your aunt has in mind?"

Jamaica made a supreme effort to think. "My sister had a large wedding last April and, er, no, Lord Clare, I don't know how long it takes."

His eyes grew bright and sly. "Sister, you say? You have a sister? Is she a de Bowen?"

"Yes—or at least she was until she married."

"And was she married from Camberleigh?"

"No, from Taunton."

"Ah, there you see!" He said triumphantly, "It is not after all, *de rigueur*."

Jamaica suspected she had missed some vital link in the chain of the conversation. "Yes, quite, Lord Clare," she said uncertainly.

He leaned forward and cocked his head intimately toward her across the lacquered table that stood between them. "Miss de Bowen, not to put too fine a point on it, I believe that your aunt is conniving something. She has fobbed me off with the weakest excuses in order, I fear, to secure another match for you."

"Oh, no! I assure you there are no other suitors. None."

He uncrossed his legs and gripped the kerchief between his knees. His hand went to his waistcoat and he drew out a slim buff envelope. "Then I suggest, my dear, that we do as we agreed to do in the first place: marry at St. Margaret's at the first available opportunity."

He slapped the envelope importantly across his knees, then handed it to her. "This is the marriage license. Nothing else is necessary but a bride and a groom and an appointment with the bishop."

She did not bother to open the envelope; she did not doubt his word, and it was a relief to be told what to do. She had felt like a lap dog without its mistress since Aunt Kate had left. "As you wish, Lord Clare. My gown will be ready on Saturday morning."

"Then, if you agree, I shall ask the bishop if he can marry us on Saturday afternoon. I'm sure he will be free. His calender is not crowded at this time of the year."

She nodded a wordless assent. He took his leave like a man with a mission, surprisingly energetic for his years.

She had a sudden urge to be out of doors, although the dinner bell would be going any minute. She rang and waited for Osgood to appear.

"My apologies to the cook, Osgood. I won't be in for dinner after all. I'm going out to take the air."

"Shall I bring the gig around, miss?"

"No, I shall go on foot. I'll be back—in time for supper, I suppose."

She decided her walking shoes would be best, the dark brown she had worn so often to take the children to Kensington Gardens. She walked across Grosvenor Square, along Piccadilly and over to Coventry Street and kept going until she reached the Charing Cross Road. From there a broad thoroughfare led to the new bridge spanning the Thames: a splendid structure. It was only a month old, and named for the site of the great decisive victory: Waterloo Bridge. It was a triumph of engineering and she had followed its progress with the children for months. She had promised they would walk over it together the day after it opened. But they were in Dorrington by then. . . .

IT HAD BEEN A MISTAKE TO GO OUT but she knew the numbness would return if she did not venture out again, and slowly she retraced her steps toward Waverly Terrace. *Madame will bring the gown the day after tomorrow*, she told herself gently. She would have only Friday to get through. Just one more day, then she would never have to feel anything again.

CHAPTER FIFTEEN

GREVILLE WAS DRESSED more for the carriage than for horseback: the white lawn shirt and stock were freshly laundered, the light gray nankeens and matching waist-coat well pressed. But he wore no coat or hat, and the morning stubble shadowing his jaw showed the extreme haste of his toilette.

Outside the carriage house, Chalmers was polishing the brass trim on Lady Camberleigh's phaeton. Greville passed him with a quick nod. When he strode into the stables, a wave of impatience overcame him at the thought of waiting for Jobe to harness the post chaise. Jobe was in the end stall showing a new stable boy how to muck it out. Instead of calling him, he went himself to the harness room and picked out a light saddle and harness. Then he walked past the stalls and stopped when he came to Winner, the swiftest horse he owned. He saddled up the horse and was mounting in the court-yard before Jobe came out and saw him.

"Going to London," he called to Jobe over his shoulder, "Tell Renfrew." And he was off, racing across the paddock, across the south lawns toward the gate, leaving Jobe openmouthed.

It was not until he was a scant mile from Lough-borough that he realized Winner was not rightfully his. The fleet two-year-old, foaled from his own stock, had just been sold to Jeremy Quester, a sporting man from

Broughton, and Quester was due to have the animal picked up this very morning.

Meticulous in his business dealings, he nevertheless shrugged the problem off. He would square it with Quester later; he had come too far to return now. But he wouldn't abuse the beast; he would change mounts. He drew rein slightly and took the rest of the road into Loughborough at a moderate canter.

He made straight for the Grateful Gander, where he knew he could trust the stables, and exchanged Winner for a post horse.

While Greville waited for the animal to be saddled, he walked into the parlor of the Gander and through a door to John Crackling's office.

"Johnny," he called to the heavy-set, grizzled innkeeper behind the desk, "I've just left out back the finest two-year-old ever raised at Foxspur. I don't know when I'll be back, but he'd better be in fine fettle. Treat him as you would your first love."

By dint of changing horses every twenty miles, the hamlets and towns flew by at courier speed. Leicester, Kettering, Market Harborough, Milton Keynes. He rode through the night and into Saturday morning, and came at last to the Marlborough Arms in Watford. Here he took a room and finally lay down to rest. One look at the small mirror on the dressing table told him that he would sweep no lady off her feet looking like this.

A limp exhaustion overcame him as he thought of the enormity of his task—and the improbability. Through the hours of riding his moods had swung up and down.

Filled with purpose when he left Lady Camberleigh, he had no thought of failure. He had not even tarried long enough to ask how much time he had. Vaguely he remembered the mention of a wedding gown in their conversation...some debts to be paid. Perhaps he had a week or two, but his blood told him to hurry.

Now, as his pulses slackened off from the hours of hot-paced riding, his optimism ebbed away.

She had been so cool, so self-possessed in his study that day, so determined not to spend another night under the same roof. And how could he blame her? He had acted like an idiot.

She had made his heart skip a beat the very first time he saw her, on the Tor Bay coast road. But he had sworn it would never happen to him again. Never. No more beautiful women, or vulnerability or festering wounds. So he had protected himself, distorting his inclinations into the most offensive travesty of normal behavior. He became a tower of disdain, doing everything he could to make her hate him.

Now he was calmly proposing to make her melt in his arms. Insanity!

But he had done it once. She had melted in his arms, he would swear it, when he kissed her. If only he hadn't hidden his burning jealousy of MacFarland and twisted his feelings so atrociously.

The memory of her in his arms quickened his pulses once more, and his drowsiness evaporated. He sprang from the bed and called for shaving water and a bath.

As he soaped before the mirror, it occurred to him that perhaps she hadn't melted after all. It was just wishful thinking on his part. Perhaps she felt nothing but disgust for him, and was limp only from shock at his audacity. Perhaps....

He took hold of himself. He was half a day's ride from Waverly Terrace and stupid with fatigue and hunger. Well, if thoughts of the governess gave him no rest, he would at least set some food in his stomach;

then perhaps he could think more clearly about his next step.

The dining room of the Marlborough Arms was not busy. At noon, the management was happy to find him a table and serve up a lamb stew.

Only three of the eight tables were occupied aside from his. On the other side of the room, at a table under a high window, sat a solitary man. His back was to Greville who could see only the stalwart shoulders clad in dark blue, emerging on both sides of the slender spine of the chair. The extrusion at the top of the chairback forming a cushioned headrest, obscured the man's head. A bright shaft of sunlight pierced the unshuttered window and fell on the blue shoulders. There was something disturbing about them.

Greville watered his wine lest he became drowsy again, and found his eyes drawn to the anonymous shoulders. At first there was just the uneasy suspicion. Then he was aware that his appetite was gone, that his ears pounded. His forehead was an anvil at the mercy of a remorseless hammer. Perspiration trickled down his back. It was those shoulders. He tried to look away and could not. When he could endure it no longer, he rose from his chair and started across the room. He froze as the shoulders turned.

MacFarland beckoned to a passing potboy. "Be a good fellow and shutter the window." He turned back to his dinner, then looked once more over his shoulder. "Greville, by all that's holy!"

It was the same damned affable tone; for all the world as if this were a pleasant encounter of friends.

Greville felt the blood drain from his face as he moved toward MacFarland's table and dropped into the empty chair facing him.

With a conciliatory smile and a head shake, Mac-Farland tilted back in his chair and raised his hands. "No muskets, for pity's sake, Greville. At least not until I've had some of this excellent pudding." He took a hearty spoonful of steamed pudding, then looked across at Greville knowingly.

"Well, well, well. First I dog your footsteps, and now you dog mine. I trust you don't own any part of this establishment? I should hate to be accused of invading your territory again."

"Have you seen her?" It was not necessary to mention a name.

MacFarland raised an eyebrow. "What is it to you?"

"She is out of bounds to you. Not to be trifled with."

"I beg to differ, my friend. She is a delight to trifle with." MacFarland's eyes danced. "She is a connoisseur's dream, beautiful, spirited—and too independent to marry. She is the ideal object for dalliance."

With supreme effort Greville suppressed a fierce urge to lean across the table, grab him by his collar and shake him until his head fell off. "She is to be my wife," he whispered murderously. "And if you ever approach her in person, by letter, or messenger—if you ever come within a hundred miles of her, I will kill you."

MacFarland dropped his spoon into the dish with a clatter. "Good heavens, man. Whyever didn't you say so in the first place? The thought never entered my head that you and she—" He shrugged. "I thought you were finished with beauties. I swear to you I have never laid hands on her—though not from want of trying. But now...well! Far be it from me to play fast and loose with the future countess of Dorrington."

"Such sensibilities never stopped you with Stella."

"My dear Greville, Stella was fair game for any

marksman long before I had the pleasure. Even you admitted it when you canceled our duel.''

"Yes, I'll admit it," he said after a pause. "And will you admit once and for all that you have a daughter?''

He watched MacFarland's features move from a placating smile to frowning concern. "That's insanity and you know it. Stella and I were together only once. Four days at my family's shooting box in Dumfries—a full two years before Caroline was born."

"Have you forgotten about your rooms off the Strand? Your love nest?''

MacFarland slapped the table, his face clearing. "Of course! You never knew the details." He sat back at ease, grasping his tankard and idly swirling the dregs of his ale. "On that famous occasion, we had the name but not the game." He cast a quick glance at Greville then watched his ale. "Oh, come. You know I only lie to women. Oh, yes, we spent the three days in my rooms sure enough. But Stella was ill. She spent the entire time in my bed, plagued with nausea. I spent both nights on my man's cot—and most of the days at the apothecary, purchasing one nostrum after another to ease her distress. Quite a messy love nest it was by the time she left. And by that time it was obvious what ailed her. After all, she had never vomited in her life. She told me. And certainly she never suffered a moment's discomfort from a guilty conscience."

The waiter placed a platter of Stilton and crackers on the table, and MacFarland tackled them with undiminished appetite.

He shook his head briskly and spoke through a mouthful of crackers and cheese. "No, my friend. If there were ever two things I was sure of that Sunday morning when she took off, it was, one, that she was in the family way, and two, that it wasn't my doing.''

"It wasn't your doing—so you ran off to sea?"

"My purse was thin. You will remember, Greville, at the time I was heir to nothing but an inadequate allowance." He washed down the cheese with the last swallow of ale and set the tankard down with a decisive thump. "Look here, if you'll take my advice, you'll assume the child is yours. She probably is, if you consider all things." He grinned wickedly. "Truth is stranger than fiction after all."

"It's possible," Greville said dryly. "But I meant what I said earlier. I will kill you, MacFarland, if you give me cause."

MacFarland met his gaze frankly. "I don't doubt it for a minute. I am aware that it was Stella's reputation and your fair-mindedness that changed your plans last time." He leaned forward earnestly on his elbows. "I'm going to tell you something—something I wouldn't have known for all the tea in China. Not because I owe it to you, but to protect my life and limb, quite frankly." He let out a long breath. "I have a wife."

Greville stared at him in astonishment.

"Oh yes, you can believe it. You see the Kilgallen inheritance came with my great-uncle's ward, Mathilda." He grimaced. "It was part of the bargain. She's a gray mouse, Greville. She looks exactly like her name suggests. By nature a lifelong spinster. Now she is mistress of Kilgallen and content never to leave the place. I intend, of course, not to let this interfere with my career of gallantry—but you will always be able to ruin it for me with a word, if you choose."

"How long have you been married?" Greville asked suspiciously.

"Since last December." He stopped to indulge in a private irony. "Mathilda was my Christmas box." He shook his head sadly. "It is really I who should bear a grudge, Greville. The fair Jamaica was in my sights. I had stalked her for a year. You have no idea what skills, what patience, what wiles I used. The children defended her virtue like dowager dragons. You should be grateful for that. But given time, I might have won. But I'll never know now, will I? I give you your future wife intact—and a weapon to use against me all my days." He extended his right arm across the table. "Will you shake my hand, Greville?"

"No, I will not," Greville said, and left in search of a hackney.

CHAPTER SIXTEEN

IT WAS ONE THING, thought Cora, staying on here to do for Her Grace's niece; it was another altogether to take over the family decisions. Any way you looked at it, it wasn't any of her business. Still, she was stuck with it now; in a right pickle.

It was two messages delivered to Waverly Terrace that had set her down in the middle of things like this—the messages, and the girl being so funny about it.

On Friday afternoon Standish came by to say he would be over Saturday at three to fetch Miss Jamaica to St. Margaret's Church in Marylebone in time for a four o'clock ceremony, for the bishop had said he would marry them then.

The second note had come early this morning, and Cora, on her way up from the kitchen with hot chocolate, had brought it to Miss Jamaica. The latter sat up in bed and read the note while Cora poured the chocolate. Jamaica's eyes got as big as saucers when she read it, then she crumpled up the paper and squeezed it so hard, her knuckles went white.

"Whatever's the matter, Miss Jamaica? Not bad news, I hope?"

"*Madame* cannot finish the gown by this morning. It will be late this afternoon." She spoke in the same voice she might have used to break the news that her whole family was drowned at sea.

"Oh, dear, miss." Cora offered her the chocolate and wondered if there was anything proper enough in the girl's wardrobe to make do with.

Miss Jamaica just sat there, letting her hold out the cup, clutching the note to her bosom with both hands. Just frozen she was. Like a startled hare. "What shall I do?" she said at last.

"Well, for a start, miss, you could take your hot chocolate," Cora said sensibly.

But Jamaica just stared at her, so she put the cup down on the tray.

"Help me, Cora. Please! I'm lost!"

She sounded just like a little waif. Didn't she have a grain of noggin, this one? Her Grace was fond of saying, *Jamaica is the clever one, the jewel in the family crown.* If she was the jewel, it didn't say much for the whole bunch of them. She was the pip more like it. But she kept her thoughts properly to herself.

"Well, Miss Jamaica," she said after some thought, "the way I see it, you've got three choices. You could send word to his lordship that you cannot be ready by three o'clock, or we could find you something else to wear instead of the wedding gown, or you could send over to Madame Veronique's that you just must have the dress this morning, and no nonsense."

"Oh yes, of course, do it," she said with relief.

"Do which, miss?"

"Those things you said—whatever you think best."

Cora recognized she'd been shoved upstairs and no mistake. What else could she do? Her Grace could not be consulted. She was supposed to consider Miss Jamaica her mistress in the absence of Her Grace. Some mistress she was turning out to be.

Cora knew pretty much what was up. She never got it

from Her Grace, of course, but word of the family do-
ings traveled downstairs fast at Camberleigh. Miss
Jamaica was saving the Canwood branch of the family
by a wealthy marriage because Canwood was a fool with
money. Lady Camberleigh had a real soft spot for Miss
Jamaica and was going to do her proud with a fancy
wedding. If the girl and the old man had decided to
forget the fancy wedding and be married quick, here in
town—well, it wasn't her place to stop it. She was just
there to look after her things, such as they were, and do
her hair.

She took her dilemma into Miss Jamaica's dressing
room, where everything she had in her trunk when she
arrived was hung on a wooden rod. It wasn't much; just
a few sad-looking things. No style, no pretty colors. All
plain and dowdy. A quick look through was enough. It
was clear there wasn't a thing she could decently stand
up in at St. Margaret's. Why, she wouldn't even be seen
in one of those herself, on her day off. Of course, she
thought, the girl would go along with anything she
picked out. She was in such a pother she wouldn't even
notice. But Her Grace would surely get to know of it,
and then she'd catch it. She quaked at the thought. If
only Her Grace were here to take over! A duchess far
outranked a marquis. She could almost hear the plum-
my voice. *Nonsense, Arthur! The child must be properly outfitted for the occasion. Simply tell the bishop we
are not quite ready.*

But she wasn't a duchess, just in service to one. She
couldn't go telling a marquis to wait. Something like
that would have to come from Miss Jamaica. Hopeless!
She was acting like a gibbering idiot, too scared silly to
do anything.

The only thing left was the fancy dressmaker. Now

there, she felt up to it. As personal attendant to a duchess for twenty years, Cora felt quite equal to handling a tradeswoman, even if she was French and had her own carriage. She'd just have to finish it in time. That's all. She could handle a needle and thread; she'd sit there herself and pitch in if need be.

Ten minutes later she was on her way down Waverly Terrace to Madame Veronique's atelier, twenty minutes' walk away.

It was after one when she returned. She'd missed her dinner but the dress was done. She rode back beside *madame*, who held the large linen-wrapped bundle draped over her lap.

CHAPTER SEVENTEEN

THE LITTLE FRENCHWOMAN SAT ON THE CARPET and put a despairing hand over her eyes. "I do not believe, *mademoiselle*, I simply do not believe!" She uncovered her eyes and winced at the drooping silk that hung sadly about Jamaica's waist.

"All morning I work with my seamstresses. Your maid, she implore me to finish by two. You must 'ave it by two, she say." She raised her shoulders to her ears, her palms held out flat. "And 'ere we are losing your waistline again. Nothing but wrinkles!"

"I see no wrinkles to speak of, *madame*."

Ever since Cora had rushed into the house twenty minutes ago with *madame* in tow, she had felt the blessed numbness wearing off. Desperately she strove to anesthetize herself, to induce the trancelike state that had carried her painlessly through the days. She stared into the mirror at the dressmaker. "Let it be. It will have to do."

"*Mais non, non, non.*" *Madame* thumped the carpet emphatically. "Never!" She turned to Cora who stood goggle-eyed behind them. "What you think?"

"Terrible. Looks like a sack."

Madame got to her feet. "*Zut alors!* This is the last time. The very last time." She went to the linen wrapper on the bed and lifted out a snippet of turquoise silk. She held it out to Cora. "Go find a 'aberdasherie. Get some thread of this color."

As Cora left the room on her errand, the dressmaker dropped to her knees again at Jamaica's feet and spoke through clenched teeth. "I will pin it again and again, until it is just so. As perfect as every Veronique gown."

Jamaica saw the dreaded pincushion emerge once more from *madame*'s large reticule. She sagged limply against the pier glass, resting her forehead on the cool smooth surface with her eyes tight shut.

"Upupup, *mademoiselle*. Stand straight if you please. There is no time for rest."

The woman was indefatigable. At the brisk tone Jamaica straightened up and felt that the tenuous threads that bound her to sanity would snap any moment. Slowly, as she was bidden, she turned full circle, stopping at every quadrant on command until she was once more facing full into the looking glass.

Confronted by her own image again, she began to examine her face with detached curiosity. Who was this mannequin with the stiff, straight back, arms held out to the side, head up, and face wiped clean of all expression? She watched as a tear formed slowly at the corner of one eye—*her* eye, she thought curiously. It welled up and the image began to blur; it spilled over as the image sharpened, and rolled leisurely down toward her mouth, leaving the lower lashes wet. She blinked, and the upper lash glistened, too. A sigh, half sob, came wrenching up from somewhere deep inside the turquoise silk.

"Stay still! Still! We are almost finished. *Voilà!*" The dressmaker got to her feet and circled slowly around Jamaica, her eyes sweeping the gown minutely from neckline to hem. Satisfied, she began to undo the tiny pearl buttons at the back of the dress. "Don't move, *mademoiselle*. Beware the pins, very sharp. In a moment I 'elp you take it off, then you can rest."

"No! Leave it on." There was such clear-cut authority in the man's voice that for an instant the dressmaker froze.

"Leave us," came the voice from the door. "I must have a word with Miss de Bowen in private."

Jamaica whipped around to face Greville, marshaling her wits like a veteran general under fire. "Stay," she ordered the Frenchwoman.

Madame, too, could stay cool under fire. In the life of a couturiere, crises were commonplace. She turned to look at the intruder framed in the doorway, appraising him instantly. His clothes were dirty, creased and torn, but her practiced eye knew a Bond-Street shirt when it saw one, no matter the condition. The cut of the nankeens was unquestionably Savile Row, and the boots, although the dust of the road clung to them, were soft hand-stitched leather. He was no highway Johnny, this one. No burglar. He was a gentleman of rank. Besides, he had called the girl by name. Was he perhaps the reason for *mademoiselle*'s wasting away?

"Stay right where you are, *madame*," Jamaica repeated.

But *madame* was French. Whatever was about to take place, she was far too discreet to witness it. She held up one finger to the stranger and gave a little nod. Then she quickly reclosed the pearl buttons at the back of the dress, whispering into Jamaica's ear, "I'll be back as soon as you are alone." Then she gathered her skirts, brushed past the man and disappeared.

Greville walked into the room and closed the door quietly behind him.

In spite of *madame*'s defection, Jamaica felt suddenly, unambiguously in command of herself as she took in his disheveled appearance. He looked like a highwayman after a hot chase. "Don't take another step!" She stood rigid, her hands balled into tight fists.

But he ignored her words and strode toward her.

"This is my bedroom, sir."

He shrugged. "I cannot think of a more appropriate place to—"

"Out," she shouted, moving quickly toward the bell cord by her bed, "before Osgood comes up and forcibly ejects you."

Instantly he was beside her. He grasped her arm and held it immobile, an inch away from the heavy silk cord.

"I have seen Osgood," he said mildly. "I am by far the better man. However, since I have no wish to embarrass you before the servants, I—"

"I have precisely twenty-five minutes to be ready for my wedding. If you do not leave this instant, I shall scream bloody murder and the devil take my embarrassment and your reputation."

He dropped her arm. "In that case, I shall leave instantly and go straight to Mayfair and inform the marquis of Clare that his blushing bride has been the common-law wife of Andrew MacFarland these past twelve months. And that will be the end of the de Bowens and the Canwoods."

She fell limp against the wall in horror. He knew everything after all! Aunt Kate had lied to her. But MacFarland—surely he didn't imagine.... "If you know so much about me, you must know that that is a wicked falsehood."

"False or true, it will serve my purpose admirably; and so, it is what I shall say."

She didn't doubt it for a moment; he was quite capable of spreading the calumny.

"You unutterable blackguard! I believe you would."

He smiled warmly. "Quite right. Now be a good girl and come down to the hackney outside. We can talk there privately. I will only take five minutes of your time."

"Whatever you have to say to me, you will say here."

"But this is your bedroom, as you pointed out. It will scarcely do for a bride to—"

"I am not leaving this room. *You* are," she said, trembling with rage. "Get out."

He gave a half bow and began to retreat. "Very well, Miss de Bowen. It is to be the marquis then, and forget about your wedding and your stepfather's debts. You can be of no further use to him." He opened the door to leave.

"No, wait...."

He paused, his back to her. His shoulders moved as he inhaled slowly. "In my hackney." His voice was low, like distant thunder.

She followed him quickly down the staircase and out through the front door where a hackney carriage was pulled up to the curb. He opened the near door and gestured her to enter. As he climbed in after her, he called out to the driver, "Marlborough Arms in Watford," then sat beside her and slammed the door.

"*What!*" She was thrown back against the upholstery as the coach took off at breakneck speed.

"It is an inn," he said, relaxing back on the cushions beside her.

"Oh, no, you don't." Her hand shot out to the handle of the door nearest her as the vehicle swung alarmingly around the corner into Grosvenor Square. He was too quick and too strong for her. He pressed her gently but firmly back into the seat.

"Oh, yes, I do," he said, holding her shoulders fast

against the back of the seat. Silently he cursed the pins. He ached to sweep her into his arms, but she was bristling with the damned pins. He was like to perforate her or himself. Aloud, he said, "Lady Camberleigh has selected you to be my countess, and so you shall."

"Over my dead body." She pressed her head deep into the cushion and tried vainly to push him away with her palms.

When he judged their speed was too fast for her to attempt jumping out, he released her and sat back.

"I hope it won't come to that," he said gently.

"I assure you it will. Stop this carriage immediately."

"Not until you've heard me out."

The hackney careened around the square into Park Lane, then bolted down the straight stretch scattering all other traffic in its path.

She must get the side glass open and scream through the window to stop the driver, she thought. She turned and stretched her hands out to the glass and pushed down. As it began to yield he captured her wrists in one hand and raised it closed.

Lightly, impersonally, he held her wrists, preventing her from trying again. "You are only prolonging your captivity, Miss de Bowen. If you were to apply that admirable mind of yours, it would become very clear to you that you have no alternative but to listen to me."

With a burst of angry strength, she pushed her wrists wide apart and shook off his hands. "Don't touch me. Speak your piece and get it over. I will stay still provided you do not lay a hand on me."

She was hard as ice. He fell back against the cushions discouraged and looked heavenward. "Oh, Lord, it's all wrong. It wasn't supposed to be like this," he muttered. He closed his eyes for a moment and renewed his efforts to stay calm and masterful. Her very proximity made it hard to breathe. When he spoke again, his voice was even and controlled.

"Miss de Bowen, I want you to be my wife."

Her hand went to her throat and she half turned her head as if she were about to be sick. "Oh, yes, of course you do. I am plain and serviceable—and you have a written guarantee from the duchess that I will suit your revolting purposes to a tee. Everything you require. I am no fashionable beauty, and my bloodline is just right for the Greville stable." She turned back to look at him, her eyes blazing. "I will see you in hell first."

"Rubbish!" he snapped, finding it hard to control his own anger. "You are beautiful enough to torment me with doubt. The only serviceability you have ever demonstrated is as a children's governess—and as for the duchess, the only thing she guarantees is that you will give me a devil of a hard time. How right she is! Bloodlines, indeed. I couldn't give a tinker's damn for your cursed bloodline. That you are niece to a duke of the realm is a gratuitous fact that I wish to God were otherwise, so that I could prove to you—" His voice dried up.

"Prove what?"

"Prove to you—" he croaked, then stopped. His throat was dry as sand, his tongue was suddenly too big for his palate, and his lips were stiff. He struggled to get the words out.

"How m-much I. . .love you," he finished painfully.

"What a travesty! You love me? You can't summon that most elemental feeling of love for your child; you're incapable of love. How dare you speak the word!"

"But I will say it." Mercifully the equipment of

speech was restored. "I have loved you since I first saw you on the Devon road when we almost collided."

"Ha! I should have known at once. You were so tender, so concerned for my safety."

"Damn you to hell, woman! Can you not see how devilish hard this is? Love for a woman—" he spoke haltingly again "—for years I regarded it . . . something to be avoided at any cost." He buried his head in his hands. "I struggled against it. I deceived myself. I disguised it by any means at hand. I did not want the hurt of it again."

She listened, almost tempted to compassion. His distress was very real. When she replied her tone was gentle. "Then, by all means, you should avoid it now. By the simple precaution of returning me this instant to Waverly Terrace. By four o'clock I am to be married. I can never cause you further hurt."

"It's too late." He lifted his head and fixed her eyes with the burning intensity of his. "Married to him, you will never cease to be a thorn in my side." He swept her hands into his and pressed them together, forming a steeple with his fingers.

"Jamaica, don't."

She let her hands rest in his.

"For God's sake, don't marry him."

She remained silent, staring at his hands, fascinated by the curious arrangement of his fingertips.

"If you can marry him for money, can't you marry me for money? It makes more sense."

"Why?" She could not draw her eyes away from his fingers.

"We're alike. We belong together. We have the same attitudes; the same interests; the same temperament."

"We are both headstrong, which means I would never

submit to you, nor you to me. That is an impasse, not a marriage.''

The hands pressed harder. "It would be an impasse I would welcome with all my heart.''

Of course! It was the fingertips. The left hand was shaped exactly like Caroline's.

She pulled her hands free abruptly. "Hold up your left hand,'' she demanded.

He obeyed without question, holding up his palm as if about to swear an oath.

"You have a strange configuration of fingers.''

"Huh?'' He scowled in confusion.

She touched the three middle fingers in turn. They were of identical length.

"Oh, that. It is a kind of hallmark of the Grevilles,'' he said impatiently. "My grandfather had the same oddity. If it bothers you—I'll have these two lopped off to normal length. Is that what bothers you?''

She smiled slowly. "Don't be ridiculous. I don't need that for a reason. I have grounds aplenty for refusing you. We are really too disparate.''

"Name me a disparity, and I will correct it.''

"Caroline! I adore the child and you cannot stand the sight of her.''

"I shall learn to love her for your sake.''

"It's not enough. You must love her for *her* sake. And for your own.''

"I shall, I swear it.''

"Then there is travel. I love to travel and you hate it.''

"I don't. I merely had my fill of Europe during the wars. If travel is your wish, we shall travel the seven seas together.''

She sighed contentedly. "It's quite impossible. We

are in constant disagreement. We argue all the time."

"I would rather argue with you than agree with any other woman." He looked at the rows of pins on her dress, and cursed them to hell.

It was a long ride to Watford, even at this maniacal speed. They argued all the way until the air in the carriage was charged with conflict. But as they reached the Marlborough Arms, their differences were exhausted. They lapsed into a mutual silence.

He took her by the hand and led her to the small room he had hired that morning. Jamaica was too spent and too hungry to protest.

"And also, will you for pity's sake stop calling me Lord Dorrington?" he said as he closed the door. His arms ached to hold her.

"What should I call you, then?" She was sick of arguments. If he touched her now, she knew she would not pull away.

"My name is Charles." His voice hoarsened as he swept her up, unable to stay his arms a moment longer.

Her hands clasped behind his neck and she pressed herself to him shamelessly.

"Ouch!" She felt the stab at her waist and ribs.

They had both forgotten the pins.

He began removing the pins carefully, one by one. "I swear I will never hurt you again."

The pins safely removed, he embraced her again until they were both breathless. Reluctantly he released her and looked at the turquoise silk drooping loosely around her slender waist. "It's a sad excuse for a dress, but it's a wedding gown. Let's use it." He took her hand and raced out of the room.

There was another harum-scarum ride through the city in search of a prelate who would waive the banns.

They were an ill-assorted pair, she thought, he in his torn shirt sleeves, she in her elaborate baggy gown; enough to arouse suspicion in any upstanding man of the cloth. But for fifty guineas, she learned, the Church of England could be quite flexible about preliminaries and turn a decidedly blind eye.

When they returned to the inn, it was with the knowledge that they could pick up a marriage license at ten o'clock the following morning, and be wedded on the spot.

He took her to a private dining room on the second floor and ordered supper. They sat behind the curtains, letting the meal cool, their eyes never straying from each other. Since the wild ride from London to Watford, they had not argued, hardly spoken at all.

Jamaica broke the silence. "There is something I must know before tomorrow."

"Anything," he said.

"Do you blame Caroline for Stella's death?"

He looked startled. "How could I? Stella died in a riding accident. It had nothing to do with Caroline."

"I see." She searched his eyes. "You must have loved her very much." For the first time, she felt the pain of jealousy.

He reached across the table for her hand. "I fell in love with her beauty. I was very young. I lived to regret it bitterly." She felt his hand close convulsively on hers. "I never want to speak of it again. You are Caroline's mother from this day. And only you."

"And you are her father."

His hand relaxed into a warm grip, and he smiled. "If that is what you wish."

Gravely, she reached for his left hand. "I do not

wish," she said. "One does not wish the sun would rise every morning. One simply knows it will."

In response to his mystified look, she grasped his three middle fingers.

"Caroline's hand is soft and little and plump—not at all like yours. But this—" she stroked the even length of each finger "—this, she could only have inherited from her *natural* father."

"What?" He was drowning in waves of sensuality that rose at the mere touch of her hand. He was utterly lost.

She gave his hand a little shake. "Charles! Stupid, stubborn, cruel, dearest, dearest Charles! She has these fingers, too. Formed just like yours. As like as peas in a pod. You shall confirm it with your own eyes when we return to Derbyshire."

He withdrew his hand. Slowly his face drained of color. "You're sure?" he asked. Jamaica nodded. For long moments he sat silent, struggling with the profound shock. It was overpowering, the impact of simply knowing the truth after all these years of doubt.

Then, stricken, he whispered, "I never noticed. How can I ever forgive myself—ever atone—for my callousness toward my own daughter."

"Simply accept her and love her, Charles." She smiled gently and added, "You'll find it quite easy to love a child with such an unusual left hand."

But she knew he would not forgive himself as easily as she could forgive him. He was suffering the most wrenching remorse. Whatever harshness he had visited upon Caroline, she could see how bitterly he repented, and she could only guess how tenderly he would devote himself to healing the breach.

She was seized by a longing to take him in her arms

and comfort him with her love. She looked down at their untouched food. Neither of them could swallow a mouthful. Their eyes met, and he smiled, guessing her thoughts.

"Shall we go?" he whispered.

BACK IN HIS ROOM HE MOVED TO KISS HER, then forced himself to stop. He cleared his throat with an effort. "I am going down to hire another room. Stay here and lock me out as soon as I leave. Don't let me back in here. I don't trust myself."

Jamaica stood between Greville and the door. She put her hands behind her and felt for the key. She turned it in the lock, removed the key and held it tight in her palm.

"I won't lock you out, Charles. Never."

"I—you expect too much." His voice was constricted. "Don't expect to trust me alone in this room with you."

"I don't," she said simply.

Without a word, he took her right hand, pried her fingers loose and took the key. He went to the window and opened it. "There'll be only one master in my house, young woman. You may as well learn that now." He threw the key out of the window, far out into the summer night, then drew the curtains closed.

AS THE MORNING SUN pierced the chintz curtains at the window, she thought about her wedding gift to Charles. It would be different from any other wedding gift; something only she could give him: his daughter. There would be other children, of course, but Caroline would be the first child she gave him.

She looked down at the dear, angular face on the

pillow and touched the thick mass of dark hair. His eyes opened instantly and he drew her face down to his.

It is only just, she thought defiantly. Just and fitting. Aunt Kate had schemed and plotted and connived at her life for a year now; and all behind her back. It was right that there was something they could share behind Aunt Kate's back.

That their wedding night took place twenty-four hours before it should have was scandalous enough to remain satisfyingly secret all their days.

He held her face between his hands as if it were the most precious of treasures, and read her thoughts.

"As long as we both shall live," he said.

Enter a uniquely exciting new world with

Harlequin American Romance T.M.

Harlequin American Romances are the first romances to explore today's love relationships. These compelling novels reach into the hearts and minds of women across America... probing the most intimate moments of romance, love and desire.

You'll follow romantic heroines and irresistible men as they boldly face confusing choices. Career first, love later? Love without marriage? Long-distance relationships? All the experiences that make love real are captured in the tender, loving pages of **Harlequin American Romances.**

What makes American women so different when it comes to love? Find out with **Harlequin American Romance!**

Send for your introductory **FREE** book now!

Get this book FREE!

Mail to:
Harlequin Reader Service
In the U.S.
2504 West Southern Avenue
Tempe, AZ 85282

In Canada
649 Ontario Street
Stratford, Ontario N5A 6W2

YES! I want to be one of the first to discover
Harlequin American Romance. Send me FREE and without
obligation *Twice in a Lifetime.* If you do not hear from me after I
have examined my FREE book, please send me the 4 new
Harlequin American Romances each month as soon as they
come off the presses. I understand that I will be billed only $2.25
for each book (total $9.00). There are no shipping or handling
charges. There is no minimum number of books that I have to
purchase. In fact, I may cancel this arrangement at any time.
Twice in a Lifetime is mine to keep as a FREE gift, even if I do not
buy any additional books.

Name _____ (please print)

Address _____ Apt. no. _____

City _____ State/Prov. _____ Zip/Postal Code _____

Signature (If under 18, parent or guardian must sign.)

ROBERTA LEIGH

A specially designed collection of six exciting
love stories by one of the world's favorite
romance writers—Roberta Leigh, author of
more than 60 bestselling novels!

1 **Love in Store**   4 **The Savage Aristocrat**
2 **Night of Love**   5 **The Facts of Love**
3 **Flower of the Desert** 6 **Too Young to Love**

Available in August wherever paperback books are sold, or available
through Harlequin Reader Service. Simply complete and mail the
coupon below.

Harlequin Reader Service

In the U.S.   In Canada
P.O. Box 52040   649 Ontario Street
Phoenix, AZ 85072-9988   Stratford, Ontario N5A 6W2

Please send me the following editions of the Harlequin Roberta Leigh
Collector's Editions. I am enclosing my check or money order for $1.95
for each copy ordered, plus 75¢ to cover postage and handling.

☐ 1   ☐ 2   ☐ 3   ☐ 4   ☐ 5   ☐ 6

Number of books checked_____ @ $1.95 each = $_____
N.Y. state and Ariz. residents add appropriate sales tax $_____
Postage and handling $_____.75____
                                                  TOTAL $_____

I enclose_____
(Please send check or money order. We cannot be responsible for cash
sent through the mail.) Price subject to change without notice.

NAME_____
                    (Please Print)
ADDRESS_____APT. NO._____

CITY_____

STATE/PROV._____ZIP/POSTAL CODE_____
Offer expires January 31, 1984   30756000000

1. How do you rate _____ ?
   (Please print book TITLE)
   1.6 ☐ excellent   .4 ☐ good   .2 ☐ not so good
   .5 ☐ very good   .3 ☐ fair   .1 ☐ poor

2. How likely are you to purchase another book in this series?
   2.1 ☐ definitely would purchase   .3 ☐ probably would not purchase
   .2 ☐ probably would purchase   .4 ☐ definitely would not purchase

3. How do you compare this book with similar books you usually read?
   3.1 ☐ far better than others   .4 ☐ not as good
   .2 ☐ better than others   .5 ☐ definitely not as good
   .3 ☐ about the same

4. Have you any additional comments about this book?

   _____ (4)

   _____ (6)

5. How did you *first* become aware of this book?
   8. ☐ read other books in series   11. ☐ friend's recommendation
   9. ☐ in-store display   12. ☐ ad inside other books
   10. ☐ TV, radio or magazine ad   13. ☐ other _____
                                            (please specify)

6. What *most* prompted you to buy this book?
   14. ☐ read other books in series   17. ☐ title   20. ☐ story outline on back
   15. ☐ friend's recommendation   18. ☐ author   21. ☐ read a few pages
   16. ☐ picture on cover   19. ☐ advertising 22. ☐ other _____
                                                            (please specify)

7. What type(s) of paperback fiction have you purchased in the past
   3 months? Approximately how many?

	No. purchased		No. purchased
☐ contemporary romance	(23) ____	☐ espionage	(37) ____
☐ historical romance	(25) ____	☐ western	(39) ____
☐ gothic romance	(27) ____	☐ contemporary novels	(41) ____
☐ romantic suspense	(29) ____	☐ historical novels	(43) ____
☐ mystery	(31) ____	☐ science fiction/fantasy	(45) ____
☐ private eye	(33) ____	☐ occult	(47) ____
☐ action/adventure	(35) ____	☐ other	(49) ____

8. Have you purchased any books from any of these series in the past
   3 months? Approximately how many?

	No. purchased		No. purchased
☐ Harlequin Romance	(51) ____	☐ Harlequin American Romance	(55) ____
☐ Harlequin Presents	(53) ____	☐ Superromance	(57) ____

9. On which date was this book purchased? (59) _____

10. Please indicate your age group and sex.
    61.1 ☐ Male   62.1 ☐ under 15   .3 ☐ 25-34   .5 ☐ 50-64
    .2 ☐ Female   .2 ☐ 15-24   .4 ☐ 35-49   .6 ☐ 65 or older

Thank you for completing and returning this questionnaire.

J12345

PRINTED IN CANADA

NAME _____
(Please Print)

ADDRESS _____

CITY _____

ZIP CODE _____

BUSINESS REPLY MAIL

FIRST CLASS   PERMIT NO. 70   TEMPE, AZ.

POSTAGE WILL BE PAID BY ADDRESSEE

NATIONAL READER SURVEYS

1440 SOUTH PRIEST DRIVE
TEMPE, AZ 85266